I0538023

WINGS BENEATH WATER
by Yaasha Moriah

Copyright @ 2017 Yaasha Moriah
Published: 31 March 2017

ISBN 978-0-9892001-3-4

Print Edition

Cover designed by Magpie Designs, ltd
Photo credits: Pixabay
Textures by Sascha Duensing

Author photo on back cover
by Arkwood Photography

Published by Yaasha Moriah
Printed by CreateSpace

to the Truth-wearer
who gave me a second chance to live

ACKNOWLEDGEMENTS

Special thanks to LSC, who suggested the title "Wings Beneath Water" and started this whole adventure.

Thanks to LoriAnn of Magpie Designs, LTD. You were such a pleasure to work with and I think you did a fantastic job on the cover.

Thanks to my beta readers, LSC, BB, and LP, for helping me move *Wings Beneath Water* from a draft to a polished manuscript.

Thanks to my family for supporting my writing, even when you see little of me during the writing process. You all keep me sane.

TABLE OF CONTENTS

preface

In November 2014, I asked readers on my blog for speculative fiction title ideas. "I'll write a story to go with your title!"

One reader responded with the title "Wings Beneath Water." The idea intrigued me and I felt somehow that this was one of the stories that, like a pearl, had to be formed layer by layer over time.

I took a walk with my sister in December and asked her for ideas. She had a few, but none of them seemed to click, though I am immensely grateful to her for taking the time to listen to my rambling, overactive writer's brain and to put forth her thoughts.

I told her that the only idea that seemed to spark some interest in me was a very hazy image of a water creature with fin-like wings, like a fantasy dragon/eel, and the equally hazy scene of a young boy sprinting through a marsh, just ahead of several hunters who seek his life. (This scene was inspired by a dream I had sometime in spring 2015. True to form, that is the only part of the dream that I remember.)

Of course, my poor sister had no clue where to go with those ideas, so we both shrugged and I tried not to think of how much it bothered me that such an awesome title should be unaccompanied by an equally awesome story.

One day in February 2015, I opened a new Word document and typed, "They say that if you see wings beneath the water, you will get a second chance to live."

And suddenly, somehow, it all clicked, like gears sliding into place, a mechanism whirring to life. BAM! I had an idea. I have no idea where that first line came from, but with one sentence, it created an entire world.

I started writing. Uraun entered the story out of nowhere within the first few paragraphs. The idea of separated brothers had been percolating through my mind for a while, but I didn't expect it to show up in *this* story. However, once Uraun arrived, I liked him, and the relationship drove the story forward. Why were Risha and Uraun separated? Why did Uraun have a scar, and why did that remind him of better days with Risha? And what, exactly, *was* Risha?

I like writing to find the answers to my own questions.

Risha's purple eyes were a recycling of my purple-eyed fairies, from a trilogy I wrote when I was a teenager. (Risha, however, is not a fairy.) I like unusual and fantastical physical features, and purple is my favorite color, so—hey! Why not?

The reflections were probably another version of an idea that I explored in my novelette *Reflections.* The reflections are indicative of one's true nature, but in this story, they are not something to be avoided at all costs. I was hesitant to recycle this idea, but it seemed to fit so well, and, after all, what's the loss? Some ideas have many facets, and cannot be explored in just one work.

The shape of the final battle, however, was not something I expected. I'm not exactly sure where the idea came from, though the symbolism suggests a Biblical origin to me. I know I didn't set out to make the story symbolic at all. It just happened, and I like it better that way, because it is not contrived and artificial. I tell a story because I like the story, and if a message creeps in—well, it must have been integral to the story.

The original draft was 4000 words, but I expanded it a month later to submit to the L.

Ron Hubbard Writers of the Future contest. I had forgotten all about it until a few months later, when I received an email congratulating me. *Wings Beneath Water* had earned a Silver Honorable Mention in the contest (top 50 internationally). I expanded the story still further in 2016 and here it is, Risha's story.

Some time while I was deeply enmeshed in writing Risha's story, I wrote this about *Wings Beneath Water*:

Something about this story feels so right, like a sort of settled quietness, an assurance that this story matters, that it was worth my time.

I hope that you will find this true for you as you read it.

Yaasha Moriah
February 1, 2017

WINGS
BENEATH WATER

By Yaasha Moriah

ONE

DEEP WATERS

They say if you see wings beneath the water, you get a second chance to live. If that is true, I may live yet. If it is not true, my blood will stain these waters within moments.

The marsh mists swirl around me like transparent hands, chilling the sweat on my forehead as my footsteps explode through the murky waters. I pause, catch a gnarled branch, and lean gasping over it.

The surface of the dark waters shows the face of a boy, with round cheeks and frightened purple eyes. Will the Karagi have mercy if they see me as a child?

No. They know what I am, and they will not waver. They will remain at a safe distance, and shoot to kill. They are master bowmen. I should know. They trained me.

That was before they knew what I am.

According to the wise woman, some say it only happens when you are born in the marshes on a moonless night. Others say that it begins when a child looks into the waters and, unknown to him, the Siyeen looks back at him from beneath the surface of the waters. Still others say it is a gift given to the one who seeks truth above all else.

If a gift results in your death, is it not a curse instead?

I have lingered too long. Even as I move, some instinctive twitch saves me, for a death-breeze fans my chin and a crimson ribbon opens across my collar-bone, the warning of a razor-sharp arrowhead.

I turn, and they are there, emerging like ghosts from the mist, their long dark hair loose around their lean faces, their leather vests leaving bare their muscled shoulders. Emotions stab my stomach, for Uraun leads them, the scar upon his right cheek lit in silver by the wavering moon.

"A child?" one hunter asks, glancing quickly at the foremost of the men.

"It is an illusion," Uraun says darkly, and draws his shaft to the corner of his lips.

I cannot outrun his arrow. I have watched too many times the stumble of a woodland buck, stricken while in mid-flight by Uraun's skill. I am also tired, too tired. This hunt has taken all my strength, all my heart.

How do you run away from someone you love?

"Uraun." My voice carries across the waters. "Please."

So long as he holds his breath, he will not shoot. Experienced archers release only at the exhalation.

I stand upon a small hillock of marsh weeds. The waters beyond my feet ripple like black silk, for I have come to the edge of the deeper waters, where the bottom is invisible and the feet find no purchase. Many things that have been lost to the deep marshes.

"Uraun," I say again. The corner of my vision snags upon something, a glimmer in the water, like light reflecting upon an outstretched wing.

It is here.

Then Uraun's jaw tightens, and, plunging, I give myself to the waters. The arrow's shaft pierces my side and my instinctive gasp fills my mouth with liquid darkness.

Something smooth slides beneath my grasping fingers, then jaws clamp around my ankle and pull me downward, deep. I struggle, panic-stricken. Have I misunderstood? Did I see a wing, or only the glitter of a marsh eel's serpentine body?

I spiral downward until my mind becomes as dark as the waters around me and my breath burns and explodes in my head. Then light births, broadens, shimmers, and I rush toward it. Am I swimming down? Or up? I cannot tell.

That is when I see the face staring back at me from the other side of the water.

My face.

I know it is my face because only I among the Karagi possess eyes the color of wild irises. It is the mark of my separation.

TWO

REFLECTIONS

I turn from the water's edge where I have laid my woven trap under the surface. Strange. I thought I saw a face in the waters, my own face, but leaner and more angular, an adult face clouded with scarlet from a wounded side.

"Risha!" My mother calls. "Come say goodbye to your father."

I do not want to say goodbye to my father, but goodbyes are inevitable.

I wade ashore and jog barefooted from the tributary, up the hill, past our dome-shaped hut of woven wood and dried river clay and descend the rocky slope. My father waits by the glass-gray river near the long boat, in which other men have already taken up their paddles and await the last of their companions to join them.

My father goes to trade upriver with the neighboring tribes, a gesture of goodwill. It is a journey made only a few times a year, and it keeps a tenuous peace amongst the People of the River. My father kneels to kiss Uraun's forehead, then mine.

"Take care of your brother," he tells each of us. I do not need telling. Uraun and I are inseparable, and have been since the day my mother found me as an infant at the edge of the marshes, abandoned. Were it not for my eyes, Uraun and I could be twins, for we have the same raven hair and brown skin.

My father steps into the long boat with the sure-footedness of a man long acquainted with the roll of the water. He sits with the other traders, and raises a long paddle that dips soundlessly, then rises silver from the waters, then dips again, as the craft glides into the current and toils upriver. Two other Karagi longboats join his, staggered a little behind in a V formation like the migrating geese of autumn.

My father lifts his hand, touching two fingers to his heart, his lips, his forehead, then raising them in the traditional farewell. It is the sign of truth, truth buried in the heart, spoken from the lips, treasured in the mind. It is the sign of our people.

My father's deep voice carries over the water. "Seek truth always."

"And the truth will preserve you," the watching families reply as one.

That is when I see it, a vision that jars me from reality. In the marred reflection, every man in the boats lies dead, twisted limbs dangling over the sides, half-closed eyes frozen. Even my father.

My gaze startles up from the waters. The men in the longboats are living, but the men in the reflection remain dead.

I do not know what to do, so I am silent, but my flesh quivers.

Uraun thinks that I am weeping and touches my shoulder. I turn my face from him, for if he sees my horror, he will ask questions I do not know how to answer.

Five days later, the river returns our men.

Every one of them has been slain, and some still carry Sarudi arrows in their bodies. When Uraun and I hear the ululating wails of the women, we abandon our quest for duck eggs in the shallows and scramble toward the faster water. But father's brother sees us and runs toward us.

"No!" he says in a tone that slaps us both across the face. "Go to your hut."

He sees the protest in our faces, but his stance is firm, his tearless eyes smoldering, and he is an elder. We go to the hut, our skin rippling with fear and do not speak.

We know.

We learn later that every warrior's face has been slit from ear to lip, a sign of a warrior utterly defeated. For the living, it is a permanent mark of shame and no feats of bravery can wipe away the stigma of that disfigurement of defeat. For the dead, it is a mark of an enemy's utter contempt to dishonor a warrior's valiant acts in life by smearing his honor after death. Such a cowardly act is beyond comprehension among the People of the River. The Sarudi have not only become bold, but they have lost their honor. An enemy without honor is a fearsome thing.

It is customary for the grieving to wash their hands and faces, and to paint black at their hearts, their lips, and their foreheads. When I bend over the water bucket to wash my hands after Uraun, I see my father's face in the reflection, his eyes glazed in death, and behind him, indistinct with smoke and overshadowed by a sky like blood, I see the People of the River at war.

I have to close my eyes to complete the ritual of mourning.

The weak Peace of the River is broken.

The Sarudi, we learn, demanded a toll for passage through their waters, and our traders, knowing that the river is no one's to claim, refused to pay. The Sarudi replied with arrows and spears.

Such a clear excuse for war demands answer, so the remaining Karagi men arm themselves and go to war with the Sarudi. The women and the old and the sick remain with a few choice warriors for defense.

My mother kneels by the grave of my father day and night, and eats little, too exhausted to weep, too broken to live. Her older brother offers us a home with his family, and his wife cares for my mother and coaxes her patiently to drink a little soup every day. Uraun and I cannot speak for weeks, and our cousins leave us be. No Karagi interferes with another's sorrow, except, as in the case of my mother, to preserve life.

I often find Uraun by the river's edge, the wind lifting his long black hair like an outstretched raven's wing. His eyes are filled with pain. I cannot bear to look at him, and spend many days in the marshes, fishing with a net I have woven and knotted from long roots. The marshes are my solace. Some see only the skeletons of trees and the cloudiness of the water. I see the life of geese and ducks and frogs, and the scattered reflection of a limitless sky.

The Karagi wait, breathless and tense, until their warriors return from the battle with the Sarudi, victorious but with many dead. An uncle and two of my cousins are gone, slain in battle. The few prisoners that the Sarudi took during the battle float back to our village, mutilated horrifically.

After the funeral rites, a restless peace settles over the river like a damp mist. We know that the war is not over and some from the Karagi journey to ask the Haveddi for aid. Such negotiations can take months, we know, but secretly we all wonder if the messengers have been caught by the Sarudi. We visit the river's edge every day to see if the Sarudi have sent their bodies back to us.

The war sleeps, but we know it will wake again soon.

THREE

CHILD OF THE WATERS

"You missed."

My humiliation ebbs away when I see that Uraun is smiling. There is a taunt in the smile, but it is not of the malicious sort. Uraun likes to win these matches with the bow—and he often does—but he is always kingly in victory. Indeed, there is no shame in losing to Uraun, for he is the best bowman of the young Karagi.

"You held your breath too long," Uraun said. "You try too hard, Risha, and think too much. Feel the aim in your belly, and release your breath and the arrow at the same time."

"In my belly?" I shake my head as I stride to retrieve the bow from the skin and wood target. "I see it with my eye. That is all I understand."

"That is why you miss the mark."

I know what he means, but I do not feel weapons as he does. The arrow and bow are like a part of himself, the aim like his own sight, the flight like the movement of his own body.

Perhaps I cannot do what he does because I do not wish to. I hunt for food. I kill for the survival of myself and my people. But Uraun has the heart of a warrior and I know that he does not think of deer and beaver when his bowstring twangs and the arrow cleaves the air. He thinks of the Sarudi.

They have never earned more deadly an enemy. When we train in the use of the bow, none is so lethal an archer as Uraun. When we wrestle with the other boys, Uraun is fierce and fearless, defeating boys several years older than he. When we run through the forest, Uraun is swiftest and runs until his cheeks are streaked with foam. For my part, I enjoy the increase of my strength in all these pursuits, but I have no appetite for competition, save with myself.

I pull the arrow straight from the target to avoid harm to its head and the straightness of the shaft. We unstring our bows, strip entirely, and descend the bank to the swift and dark river, fanned by a breeze that offers no relief from the stifling heat of the summer day.

The other boys assemble naked at the edges of the waters, their brown bodies glistening with sweat and caked with dust, tired and overheated by the morning training set by the warriors.

One of the warriors hefts a white stone the size of a man's fist and throws it into the deeper, faster waters of the river. We explode into the waters before the stone has even touched the water, wrestling each other and the river for the privilege of being the first to reach the stone.

The coolness of the water stings my skin, even as I simultaneously shrink from it and revel in it. Then I submerge entirely, shuddering throughout my body, and it is like I become one with the water.

There is one thing in which I claim mastery: swimming. It is like I am made for water, and there are few things so pleasurable as to feel the water slide across my limbs like silk, bringing every hair of my skin alive with sensation.

Battling the current, eyes open in the frigid waters, lungs burning with the need for air, I spear toward the place where the stone fell. It is not so easy to find the stone in the swift-moving water and amongst the tangle of smooth rocks on the river-bed, and the search that started with vigor soon becomes as exhausting as the morning training.

Uraun and I burst above the water at the same time and Uraun curses. "Blood of the Siyeen!"

I mirror his earlier teasing grin.

"What?" Uraun growls at me.

"You must feel it in your belly."

"I do, I assure you. I have swallowed half the river." So saying, he chokes up a mouthful of water, gulps a deep breath of air, and descends again.

I remain at the surface for another few breaths. I am not in a hurry. I know I will find the stone. I always do, the same way that Uraun always hits his mark. The other boys battle and strive and fight, but I simply think like the water and move like a brown eel.

I find the white stone a minute later, a pale gleam amongst the darker stones, and emerge to hold it victoriously above my head for the warriors to see. They nod solemnly to me as the gasping boys swim back to shore and flop like beached fish upon the smooth rocks and wet earth of the shore.

I am not tired when I deliver the stone to the warrior who threw it.

I seat myself by my collapsed brother, who casts me a sharp, sideways glance, then throws his arm over his eyes to shield from the sun.

Uraun is a strong swimmer, and I know it needles him that the skill at which I excel, simply for the joy of it, he cannot match even with the force of his greatest energy.

"You are quickly becoming master of many skills, Uraun," says gray-bearded Kashik, one of the warriors. "But your brother outdoes you in the water. How long will you let the one of the purple eyes overcome you?"

Kashik is of the thought that competition breeds strength and anger fuels power, but his constant setting of the boys against each other seems to me to be a fool's efforts. It is the Karagi way for every warrior to defend his honor, but Uraun seems driven to it more than most. He needs no encouragement to competition.

Uraun sits up slowly, glances toward me expressionlessly, and regards Kashik for a long moment. The other boys watch, breathless, to see how Uraun will defend his reputation.

Then my brother speaks quietly.

"I am an arrow on land and Risha is an arrow in the water. I earn my place. *He earns his.*"

Then he rises and walks away, shedding his fatigue like a cloak because of his rising anger. I follow, match his stride, and we remain silent. The bond of our brotherhood is profaned by no spoken assurances, but all of the Karagi know that we are like two hands to the same body, inseparable and always present with the other.

When the shadows lengthen and the warriors release us from the last of our training, our muscles swollen with the blood of our exertion and our minds blank with exhaustion, Uraun and I return to the tributary where we have set our traps. The two fish we have caught are not large, but they are not plagued by the worms that sometimes infest the fish of the river. After cleaning them, we bring them back to the dome-shaped hut where my aunt and female cousin fry them on the hot, flat stones by the fire.

My mother's brother arrives soon afterward with my male cousins.

"How went the training today?" my aunt asked.

My uncle tells the story of the day's events, dwelling on the accomplishments of Uraun and I as equally as those of his own sons. When he tells the story of Kashik and Uraun, she crows with pleasure.

"Well said, Uraun!" She cuffs his cheek with affection. "It is a warrior's strength to acknowledge the skill of another warrior. And well done, Risha! Uraun is right. You earn your place."

"It is his nature," says a voice from the shadows of the hut. "He is a child of the waters."

We freeze. It is the first time my mother has spoken in months.

We hold our breaths and my mother shifts, only visible by the reflection of the firelight in her eyes.

"The water is his sight."

My uncle glances at my aunt, and I hide my face as my spine chills.

"What do you mean, Venhad?" my uncle asks quietly.

"I remember that night," replies my mother, her voice distant. "Uraun was less than a moon old and slept fitfully, but when I walked by the river beneath the moon, he quieted to be near the water. You were drawn to him, Uraun. You were drawn to Risha. You wanted me to find him."

"My mother, I was an infant." Uraun's voice is hushed, wary.

"Children *see*," my mother replies. "You saw. When I walked by the river, I saw him. The child of the waters, naked as a child from the womb. Some of the Peoples of the River place children in baskets of reeds and give them as gifts to the waters, but it had not been done so with you, Risha. It was as though you had swum there yourself. You lay in the shallows and you did not shiver and you were not drowned. You lived. And I beheld you and knew by your eyes that you were a child of the waters. I knew also that you were meant to be my son and Uraun's brother."

She begins to weep and rock back and forth. "I know you see things, Risha. I know that you saw something that day in the water when your father left. Your face changed and I saw horror upon it. What did you see, Risha?"

My heart turns to stone and I cannot speak. My mother lifts her face to me and speaks as though pronouncing a prophecy upon me: "From water you have come and to water you shall return."

All eyes slowly turn from my mother to me. My mother does not speak again but I feel her eyes pressed upon me like cold fingers.

The next morning, when my aunt goes to rouse my mother, my mother does not wake.

FOUR

The Beast in the Reflection

I feel Uraun's attention bent toward me all through the funeral rites and the burying of our mother. When the earth covers her entirely, too deep for the scavenging animals to find, my uncle cuts his thigh with his dagger and marks us with his thumb on our hearts, lips, and foreheads with his blood, the Karagi sign that we are now one blood, sons to him as surely as if we were born of his seed.

The warriors do not expect us to participate in the training on our day of mourning, but Uraun is adamant. I hear later that he was master of all challenges, as though empowered by more than a boy's strength.

I do not train, but retreat to the quiet of the marshes. There is solace in the glassy waters and the drift of the grasses.

There is also uncertainty.

"From water you have come and to water you will return."

In the evening, Uraun finds me by the place where the river and the marshlands meet. For a time, he sits quietly and watches the rise of the moon upon the nests of the herons, the whispering cattails and grasses, the sentinel wetland trees.

I know why he has come, but I wait for him to ask. I have readied the words to speak and though they seem pale and ugly, like grubs, I can find no substitutes.

"What did she mean?" Uraun whispers at last.

"I saw our father's death," I reply, afraid to look at my brother. "When he left, he and the warriors with him were live in the boats, but slain in the reflections."

Uraun was quiet for a long time. Then:

"Did you tell her?"

"No."

"Then how did she know?"

"She said she is my mother. Perhaps mother know things. But I told no one."

"Why not?"

At last I look at him, my face twisted with anguish. "What would you have me do, Uraun? I was a child. I saw something that made no sense to me. I did not know it was true."

"You *felt* it was true."

I cannot answer this, for he is right.

"Uraun, no one would have believed me if I had spoken, if I had warned them. Would you have?"

"Yes."

"You believe me because our father is already dead, because what I saw came true."

"No." Uraun's voice bites. "I believe you because you are my brother."

Again, I have no answer. Uraun's breath hisses through his nostrils and I squeeze my eyes shut.

"You blame me."

"You did not kill our father, Risha."

"I could have saved him."

"Perhaps."

Uraun looks over the haunting beauty of the marsh and something expands in his dark eyes.

"I do not know what it means," he says. "Or whether you shall ever see such a thing again, but if the reflections change for you again, tell me."

But when I see a strange reflection again, I am afraid, because this time, the reflection is Uraun's.

We are both withered with exhaustion, but the hunt has been fruitful, even though the three rabbits are small. Uraun's masterful aim through the rabbits' eyes have preserved as much of the meat as possible.

"The wise woman watches you." Uraun's voice breaks our soft footfalls upon the damp fallen leaves of the forest.

"Uraun, she watches all the doings of the Karagi. It is her right."

"No, Risha. She watches *you*. Do you not see her when we train in our swimming and in the boats? She sits upon the opposite shore and observes."

"Why should she watch me?"

"I do not know. But she has done so ever since our mother died. As though she is waiting to see something."

I glance sharply at my brother. "You do not think she knows?"

Uraun shrugs. "She is the wise woman. There is no telling what she knows."

"I have not seen anything since our father's death. There is nothing for her to observe of me."

Uraun does not reply and my words feel hollow to me. We rarely speak of my visions and then only in hushed voices and great sobriety. It is as if both of us fear to wake the eyes of vision in me.

We halt by the river to clean the rabbits, sliding our knives under the skins and parting the clinging fibers from the muscle cleanly, carefully carving out the bowel. After the long hunt, the crouching cramps my neck and I rise to stretch my back and shoulders.

Uraun remains crouched over the rabbit by the water's edge and he glances up once toward the fading orange light on the western horizon.

I suck in my breath.

My brother's reflection is gripped in the claws of a hideous creature, some nebulous shade that warps and flickers in the water, so that I cannot see it clearly. The Uraun of the reflection is twisted and crippled with pain, his face pale, and his blood seeps from beneath the creature's claws.

I blink.

No, it must be just the rabbit's blood. It must a trick of the waning light.

But I cannot unsee the reflection. It remains and my stomach coils into an acid knot. Death I can interpret, but this... What does it mean?

Uraun stirs and turns his head to glance at me, squinting. "No hurry, Risha. I enjoy doing all the work while you rest your weary bones."

I flick his ear. Laughing, I dodge his answering slap, miss my balance, and tumble backward. In an instant, Uraun scoops a handful of mud from the shallows of the river, leaps upon me, and slimes the mud over my face, into my ears, up my nostrils. I shout and choke and laugh, but I am not strong enough to fight him off, so I bite his wrist until he cuffs me a blow that sends fireflies winking through my vision. As I flail, dazed, Uraun retreats, his wrist bloody and victory dancing in his dark eyes.

"You bite me again and I will bite your nose off."

I bare my teeth in a ragged grin. "If I bite you again, I won't let go."

"As if you would have a choice," Uraun snorts, returning to the river. As he lowers himself to finish cleaning the rabbit, I kick his backside and he pitches headlong into the river with a sharp gasp and a reflexive twist. The instant his head emerges from the water, he roars.

"Risha!"

I laugh from the river side. "O mighty warrior! Lord of the fishes! King of the eels! Shall I find a swamp-grass crown for you?"

I step in the water and he knows that it is a fool's errand to chase me in my element, but his pride goads him and in a moment he is upon me, ducking me under the water, attempting blows. It is only when I have half-drowned him that he ceases to wrestle me.

We are both completely soaked and shivering in the evening air as we wind our way back through the ferns and the dogwood to the home of our uncle, the rabbits swinging from our fingers on twine.

Uraun flashes me a grin once. I smile back, but the smile is hollow.

Even amidst our warrior's play, Uraun's reflection had remained the same and the beast did not leave his back.

Over many months, as I continue to observe my brother's reflection, the reflected Uraun and the hideous creature on his back begin to merge into one and to wear a single face.

My promise to Uraun stings in my belly every time I see his reflection. Still, I hold my peace until our fifteenth year.

"Risha."

I heft the earth on the head of the shovel and cast it over the side of the ditch that will channel the spring floods away from our village. I flicker my gaze momentarily toward my brother. "What?"

"Why do you shrink from the water?"

I turn back to the earth, my gaze downcast. "Why should I shrink from the water?"

"Do not think that I have not noticed," Uraun says, leaning upon his shovel, his bare torso gleaming with sweat and his raven's feather hair clinging to his neck and forehead. "You have no love for the training in the river as you once did. You only go willingly to the river when you are alone."

I shrug. "I like solitude best."

Uraun regards me for several strokes of my shovel, then catches my arm with such ferocity that I must meet his gaze. He speaks in a hoarse whisper.

"You see something in the reflections. Something you fear. Something that, despite your promise, you will not tell me."

The fire and the hurt in his eyes smite me and I drop my gaze to my feet. "I have not known how to tell you, Uraun."

"Is the 'how' all that matters? You made a promise, Risha. Can I still trust you?"

I swallow hard.

"The reflection is yours."

Uraun's jaw muscles flex and the blaze in his eyes quickens. "Go on, Risha."

"There is a dark beast on your back, its claws grown into your flesh, and you bleed until it seems as though you must die, but you remain alive. Yet as time goes on, you and the beast have become more and more alike, your bodies fused, your faces the same. Very soon, you and the beast will be one and the same. The beast will be Uruan, and Uraun will be the beast."

I catch his arm. "Please, Uraun, cast it away. You know what the creature is and what it does to you. Vengeance brings no peace, as death cannot beget life. Death only begets death."

Uraun shakes off my hold. "What are you talking about?"

He thrusts by me, jostling my shoulder with a roughness that casts me against the wall of the ditch. He pauses for a moment, as though some sudden pain or remorse seizes him, but then he continues.

When he passes a puddle that quivers at the bottom of the ditch, the beast in his reflection has sunk its teeth into his neck until its head has begun to meld with Uraun's head. In the reflection, Uraun's face is twisted with tears and pain.

I cast down my shovel and heave myself from the ditch.

"Risha!" My uncle calls from the ditch.

I only shake my head and stride away, toward the marshes, widening the distance between myself and my retreating brother.

five

CURSED CHILD

"You cannot have wounded it as grievously as you thought," I pant, my knees half-giving way before the power of my momentum drives me forward to better footing.

"I know where my arrow struck," Uraun replies through gritted teeth, whipping a branch back in my face unheedingly. "That a creature can survive so long with an arrow in its throat is a marvel worthy of a warrior's admiration."

He pauses to lean against a tree and I nearly collide with him. He turns to me, his chest heaving, his damp hair clinging to his neck. "Halt a moment and let us catch our breath."

I have wanted him to say those words for the last three miles. I slump to the foot of a large maple tree and suck in great drafts of air, fumbling for my water-skin.

"You drink far more water than any other warrior among the Karagi," Uraun observes, crouching lightly on the balls of his feet. "It is a wonder your bladder does not need to be emptied every hour. Look. You have taken two water skins for yourself."

I chuckle breathlessly and raise an eyebrow in a taunt. "Be glad I carry more weight than you. Otherwise, I would have caught the buck by now while you strove to catch up with me."

Uraun laughs and his punch to my shoulder carries no ill-will, though it bruises just the same. My brother surveys the land around us, at the thick-trunked trees and the slender undergrowth that break the light into a thousand white and gold shards on the forest floor. He squints toward the pale gleam of the setting sun, just visible through the trees.

"We are far on the western side of the River," he says quietly.

"The Sarudi and their allies have penetrated southwestward," I recall, straightening. "Let us hope there are none in these woods."

The setting sun seems to pour the color of blood into Uraun's eyes. "I fear our prey may have led us beyond safe borders."

He does not sound fearful at all.

I press my back against the tree to lever myself into a standing position. "And how exactly shall we retrieve the buck so many miles from home?"

Uraun shrugs. "We carry it. For miles."

I groan and set my head back against the bark.

Uraun grins and prods me with a knuckle. "What is this? A warrior losing his courage?"

"Not my courage," I reply, attempting to calm the uncontrollable quivering of my spent legs. "My strength. Even the greatest warrior has an end to his strength."

"And so must a buck." Uraun pulls me fully upright. "Come, brother. It cannot be far."

Wearily, I fall into step behind my brother. As we go, Uraun points to the marks of our quarry's passing—a smear of blood on the forest floor, an imprint of a cloven hoof on the soft earth, a tuft of pale fur snagged by a twig. The buck is becoming clumsy now in its waning strength and the signs become more numerous as we close in on our prey.

At last we see it, sprawled upon the leaves, its tawny cheeks and sides sprayed with foam. The buck twitches instinctively as Uraun approaches, but its slender legs and heaving sides have nothing left to give. In a moment, Uraun slits its throat and the creature's life ebbs away.

"I will disembowel it," Uraun says. "The lighter weight will make it easier to carry. Find a pole that we can lash its legs to. We will carry it between us."

I already know what to do and have already begun my search for a straight and stout sapling, but it gives Uraun pleasure to tell me, so I let him.

As I stumble through the forest, some warning filters through my consciousness.

I smell smoke.

I turn and stagger back the way I have come, sudden terror lending me strength. Uraun rises at the haste of my approach, his knife already crimson in his hand and a question in his eyes. Then I see the man emerge from the lengthening forest shadows behind Uraun and my hand flies to the knife at my hip.

Uraun does not even have time to nock an arrow to his bow before the forest around us crackles with footsteps. From the sound of it, there are at least a dozen men, filtering into our vision like shadows turned men.

We have been fools. The Sarudi saw the buck fall near their camp and recognized the make of the arrow in its throat. They had only to wait to see who would come to claim it. Our prey has become our trap.

Uraun knows he cannot nock an arrow to his bowstring quickly enough, but he makes the attempt anyway. In an instant, the Sarudi warriors close the distance between us. I swipe with my knife—a flash of cold steel in the burning sunset—and the next moment, something explodes in my vision and I am staring at a pair of moccasins embroidered with porcupine quills in the bear pattern of the Sarudi. My head screams with a high-pitched voice.

Uraun and I are hearty lads, but we are far too spent to offer more than a meager struggle for our freedom, despite our fear. Powerful arms lift us to our feet and thrust us through the shadow-striped forest until we collapse into a circle of firelight.

Uraun and I choke for breath, our bodies pressed by our own exhaustion into the soft earth. The men bind our wrists and ankles with rough rope woven from the marshland grasses and we have nothing left to do but lie and gasp and wait for the horrors that will come.

One Sarudi warrior crouches by Uraun, his face half in flickering shadow from the nearby fire. "You are far from home, boy. What is your name?"

Uraun answers with a spray of spittle at the feet of his enemy.

"You Karagi are all the same," the warrior sighs, rising and nudging Uraun's cheek with the toe of his boot. "You have no respect for the other tribes."

"We are not maimers of the dead," Uraun snaps back.

"Watch your tongue, boy, or I shall cut it out for you."

Uraun holds his peace, but I do not have to see a reflection to watch the beast rise up in his expression. If he were unbound, no Sarudi would be safe while my brother lived.

"What about you, quiet one?" The Sarudi warrior crouches at my side and I instantly drop my gaze.

"Look up at me, lad!"

I do not obey until he slaps my cheek and forces my face to turn toward him.

"By the bear's claw," the Sarudi whispers. "What devilry is this I see? I have never seen eyes like this before."

The others come close, stooping to peer into my face. Uraun twists, fear flickering across his face, and I know that, though his heart will not quail when faced with his own danger, he feels terror for me.

"I have heard of such things," says one of the men. "It is a sign of a cursed child. That the Karagi would keep such a creature amongst them is their own undoing."

"We should kill it," says the first man, drawing a knife.

SIX

The Siyeen

Uraun explodes from the earth and it takes three men to wrestle him back to the ground.

"This one fights," one of them laughs, pulling back Uraun's head by the roots of his hair.

"For a cursed child? Strange loyalty." The man with the knife returns his attention to me.

"Stay your hand." Another warrior arrests the knife-hand. "It is not so simple to slay this kind. Even in death, the curse remains alive." He pauses, adding, "Would that I had listened better to the words of the wise woman of the Sarudi. She knew of such things, but I did not heed well. I fear to kill it and I fear to let it go."

"You fear too many things, Kaheela."

"Some things are worth fearing."

"Then we shall take it with us."

"I fear that as well, but I see no other choice."

"Perhaps," says another Sarudi warrior, "We can make the cursed thing the trouble of someone else. They are good strong lads, strong of sinew and bone and, as we have seen, excellent runners and hunters. It is not good to waste such skill when it can be to our advantage. They should fetch a handsome price upriver or we may trade them for better weapons from the Steel People."

The other men consider and murmur amongst themselves, but it seems that they agree. We would go into slavery, far away from the People of the River, where we could never again trouble the Sarudi people.

"But there is yet another way to ensure that they will not trouble us," says the man with the knife, a hunger kindling in his eyes. "Let us clip the fighting one, so that he never dares lift his hand against a warrior again."

The Sarudi man seizes Uraun's long black hair and cuts it raggedly while Uraun struggles in vain against the grip of two warriors. Uraun manages to clamp his teeth upon the wrist of one of his captors, who curses and cuffs Uraun until my brother nearly loses consciousness, but he does not let go. His teeth remain sunken into his enemy's flesh.

"You bring this upon yourself, boy," the Sarudi knife-wielder growls and thrusts the tip of the blade by Uraun's mouth. Then he draws the point up toward Uraun's ear in the desecration of shame that the Sarudi had perpetrated against our father.

Uraun's scream shudders through the forest. It is fear like I have never heard it from my brother's lips, fear not of death, but of a life of shame. I know now what my brother fears above all else.

Uraun becomes like a wild creature, thrashing, snarling. Even bound, he is like an eel of the waters and the warriors' hands grapple for a hand-hold. At last, the Sarudi hold him down, crushing his young body with their weight and strength, and twist his face toward the knife that will mark the second cheek and seal Uraun's fate as a warrior defeated.

They are cowards. They are twelve against one. They are men against a boy. To destroy a warrior's honor before he has even truly come of age as a warrior is the work of beasts, not of warriors, but they do not care. Those who would maim the dead do not care for the living.

As the Sarudi jeer and Uraun's captor presses the knife-tip close to Uraun's other ear, I writhe in my bonds.

If Uraun loses his honor, it will kill him. It will kill him. I cannot let that happen.

I forget that I am only a boy.

Suddenly, a fierce light bursts upon the Sarudi, casting their faces in a strange lavender luminance like the pallor of death. The fire swallows itself in a puff of black smoke and the purple radiance spears through the trees as though light has become a weapon.

The men turn toward me and their mouths open in soundless horror.

I feel strength such as I have never known, coursing through my veins like lightning through a dark sky. I arch my back and expand my limbs as the ropes around my wrists and ankles snap and hiss like cut bowstrings. Burning breath rises in my throat, roiling white flame that pours through my lips as I scream.

It is not a boy's scream. It is a scream that shudders the trees and makes the very air turn liquid like water, that concusses the ears of the hearers. The Sarudi cry out and fall back as I rise to my feet and shake myself.

When have they become so small and child-like?

As I whirl upon the Sarudi warriors, my shoulders ripple with power and my fingers curl and sharpen at the tips into spear-points.

In every Sarudi eye, my boy's reflection melts into that of a white creature with burning violet eyes and dark wings outspread like storm-clouds.

I am their curse.

A few recover their senses enough to seize their spears and cast them toward me, but the spear-tips glance from opalescent scales as impenetrable as steel plates and fall harmlessly to the side. I swing my head from side to side and a jet of white flame answers their assault.

The cry goes up, a cry from those who see their own death.

"The Siyeen! The Siyeen!"

Abandoning their weapons, the warriors flee like dry leaves before wind. I am a bright fury behind them, claws tearing at the earth, jaws snapping. I rake the back of one man with my claws, and he stumbles, recovers, and flees to the side, his flesh torn and bleeding through his tunic. Another Sarudi stops and fumbles with his bow, but his courage deserts him, and he turns.

The crash of his footsteps marks his flight through the underbrush.

I stand over the bleeding body of my brother and pour white fire upon the retreating Sarudi, my wings beating the air into a hurricane. Two fall and do not arise.

When the sound of the departing Sarudi no longer reach my ears, I withdraw from Uraun, huddling at the base of a tree as my fury ebbs and its heat cools in my body.

"Risha," Uraun calls softly.

The sound of his voice becomes my anchor and I feel as though I am melting into a small, defenseless creature, something with no thick hide or armored scales, with no claws and no razor teeth.

I am a boy again.

For a moment I lay on the earth, gasping, my vision smeared by tears that I do not remember permitting. I am utterly naked and feel as though I have run for days.

"Risha," Uraun calls again and I crawl to his side. The discarded knife lies close by him and I cut his bonds with shaking hands.

"Did you kill them all?" he asks, his hand rising to his bloodied cheek.

I sit back on my heels and swallow hard, closing my eyes. "I killed two."

"Why did you not kill every one of them? They are likely the same who killed our father."

"I only meant to protect."

I slump to the earth and curl my legs toward my stomach, trembling violently.

"Can you walk?" Uraun asks gently.

I cannot reply and my vision blurs so greatly that I can only sense, rather than see, Uraun's concern for me.

Uraun rekindles the fire until the heat wraps me like a blanket and my trembling subsides. My brother remains by my side, silent. When I cough, he tilts the water-skin to my lips and, when my water is gone, he gives me his own. His gentleness is almost more than I can bear.

When I wake in the morning, Uraun is still watchful. The deer has been savaged by the scavenging wolves during the night, but Uraun collects the discarded weapons of the Sarudi, spoiling their camp, and supports my weak legs on the long walk home.

It is late afternoon when we come upon a party of our kinsmen.

"Where have you been?" our uncle asks.

Uraun does not answer immediately, but delivers me into the hands of two Karagi warriors. Then he turns to my uncle with sobriety that makes him seem decades older. "There will be time enough for questions, but first, Risha needs care. He is spent."

"So are you," my cousin observes when Uraun stumbles on the way.

"I am well enough."

By the time we reach the village, Uraun is incoherent with exhaustion, responding to questions with words that make no sense and consumed with thirst. My aunt lets him drink a little warm broth to assuage his need. Then he collapses upon the furs and falls asleep instantly.

I ghost through a twilight of consciousness until the wise woman arrives, her clothing permeated with the scent of herbs and smoke. She kneels by Uraun and cleans the wound on his cheek.

"It will scar," she says in a voice like trees creaking in the wind. "But it is only one cheek. His honor remains. Let him rest for the next few days and do not let him persuade you to let him carry his usual burdens. His body is far overspent. Only at my word may he resume his training."

My uncle eyes my brother dubiously. "You do not know how difficult it will be to restrain him."

"You are a warrior. He is a boy. I am certain you will find a way."

She turns to me. "Now for you, Risha."

Her hands are gentle as she passes them over my body, seeking through touch what the eyes alone could not find. She discovers wounds I did not know I had and prescribes rest and water to heal my body.

Before she goes, she cups my chin in her hand and peers into my eyes. I feel suddenly as though I am naked to her not only in body, but in spirit, that she can read in my gaze what I do not even know of myself.

"Risha," she says softly. "When you are ready, come to my island and we will speak."

SEVEN

The Wise Woman's Story

When the elders of the tribe question Uraun and I, Uraun tells them that we encountered a Sarudi patrol while we sought a deer, that we fought them and they nearly overpowered us, and that my warrior's courage saved him from permanent shame. He was careful to preserve his own dignity and honor, but he did not diminish my part in his deliverance.

Uraun speaks nothing of my transformation, but he is a wise liar. He does not ascribe to us impossible feats that boys could not accomplish against seasoned enemy warriors, but only affirms that we possess enough skill to have escaped with our lives and honor.

Uraun knows, as I do, that they will accept his word and not dare to penetrate into the Sarudi territory to verify the details. They will not see the two burnt warriors, the singed trees, or the imprints of great clawed feet.

The Karagi are satisfied with the story, though they brood darkly amongst themselves about the evils of the Sarudi and the necessity of a Karagi victory against so unworthy a foe.

Uraun and I meet at sunset by the tributary where we often fish and sit in silence for a long time. At last, Uraun murmurs, "Is this another thing you have never told me?"

I gaze at him with reproach. "No. That has never happened before. I still do not understand what happened."

"You are not a mere boy, Risha."

I stare out over the waters and it feels as though a band presses around my chest. At last I ask in a whisper, "Do you fear me?"

"Why should I fear you? You saved me."

"But you think *they* will fear me. The other Karagi."

"Because they did not see what I saw."

"You saw a creature of death."

"No. I saw my brother."

"I was not myself."

"And what is your self but my brother? Your form does not matter."

He pauses then asks quietly, "Do you fear what you are?"

I cannot answer. He speaks as my brother, but Uraun's reflection shows the face of the beast that has become one with him.

Uraun loves me truly and his words are sincere. I know this. But he also sees my uses, that the creature that I am promises death to the Sarudi.

My chest tightens with the burden of unshed tears.

I seek the wise woman as soon as my strength returns. She waits at the edge of her marsh island as my small canoe approaches, her gray hair tucked beneath her dark hood, and she catches the rope to tie my boat to the mooring stake. It is as though she has anticipated the exact moment of my arrival.

As she leans over the water, I study her reflection. It wears the face of a much younger woman, almost a girl, and seems illuminated from inside, like sunlight through leaves. I am sure now of my purpose and follow her when she beckons me inside her hut.

The wise woman's hut is dim and smells of herbs and smoke, as she does. Drying plants hang upside-down in bundles along the wall, and an owl flutters on his perch at my entry. In one corner, there rests a roughly circular stone with a shallow impression in its center, stained with the powder of plants, which were crushed by the accompanying smooth, oblong stone.

The wise woman and I sit cross-legged on the floor, across the firepit from each other, screened in each other's vision by the pillar of smoke between us, which ascends to the open circle in the roof of the hut.

For a time, there is only the crackle of the fire, and the whisper of the owl's movements, as the wise woman waits for me to speak.

At last, suppressing a tremor, I ask, "What is a Siyeen?"

The wise woman seems untroubled by this question. "Why do you ask?"

I dare not answer. Observing my face, she says carefully, "The Siyeen is a legend among the Sarudi, and they fear it. Tell me, Risha, what is the greeting and farewell of the river people?"

"Seek truth always."

"And the truth will preserve you," she finishes. "The Siyeen is a truth-wearer. There is a Sarudi legend that explains."

Her tone changes to the lilting, sing-song quality that marks the stories of the Karagi.

It is said that, long ago, the People of the River had no clans, but were savages who killed one another and roamed the marshes for food. They had none of the honor of the warriors nor the loyalty of clans. Their bodies wore the faces of men, but their hearts wore the faces of beasts.

Among the People of the River lived a boy named Nayu, the youngest of his family. One day, he paddled in his canoe through the marshes at the river delta, the place that the Karagi now inhabit. Seeking fish to add to his family's pot, he spied what he took to be the side of a large fish, rising for a moment just above the surface in a great curve. Without hesitation, he loosed an arrow from his bow. For a few moments, the creature thrashed, but at last, the scarlet waters ceased to boil, and the dead creature rose to the top of the water.

When the boy paddled closer, he saw, to his surprise, that it was not a fish, but a long, silver-white eel with long fins upon its sides. The fins were shaped like the wings of a sky-bird, but were translucent and threw rainbows like the wings of a dragon-fly. The eyes, frozen in death, seemed a strange color for a water-creature, for they were purple like the irises of the marsh.

The boy felt sorrow for bringing death to such a beautiful creature, but, knowing his family's need for food, he hauled it into his boat with much trouble and took it home. When he prepared it for the pot, the skin came away from the bones in one piece, glimmering like an opal stone, and he set it aside. His family remarked on the delicacy of the flesh, and, though they sought another creature like it, none was found.

As for Nayu, he fashioned the skin of the eel into a cape, which he wore about his shoulders. Though he did not mark it until later, the cape worked upon the edges of his mind, smoothing it like water over stone, and he began to feel as one who has been drawn from the dead and now regards all life as a gift. His strength in battle became a thing of legend, yet his mercy—a thing strange among the People of the River—earned him more reputation amongst the people.

One day, Nayu entered the marshes to fish, as he had for so many years. Since the day was warm, he removed the eelskin-cape and placed it in the bottom of his boat, paddling soundlessly through the still waters.

A flicker of white caught his eyes, and he saw, to his astonishment, an enormous winged eel stretched in the shallows of a marsh island, of the same kind as the eel he had killed, but much larger. It was the length of seven men, and as thick around as two.

As it lay utterly still, Nayu paddled closer, and at last drew his boat upon the shore and crept to the side of the creature and ran his hand along its side. It stirred slightly and he leapt back. Now he saw that its sides rose and fell with shallow breaths, and he came to its head.

The eyes that looked back at him were like wheels of violet fire. Nayu's breath came short and his palms sweated.

"What are you?" he asked. "And why are you here?"

"I am the Siyeen," the creature answered, and its voice sounded like rain upon the river. "I am old, having lived many generations of men, and I have come here to die."

"It is not good to die alone," Nayu replied. "Have you no one to stay with you?"

"I had a child," the Siyeen rasped. "But he was lost many years ago, no doubt to some hunter of the marshes."

Nayu's heart smote him. He thought of the skin in his boat, and knew that it had belonged to the child of the Siyeen. He realized that he could stay with the Siyeen and comfort it in its loneliness, but it would be the wretched kindness of an enemy if he did not speak the truth. For a time, he wrestled with himself even as the Siyeen wrestled for breath.

At last, torn between fear and duty, he fell upon his knees before the Siyeen.

"Alas!" he cried. "I am he who slayed your child. It was done in innocence, for I believed him to be a fish, but it cost your child his life. I offer myself and my life in place of his, and will endure the judgment due a slayer."

The Siyeen raised its head from the shallow waters, and it towered above the trembling man. The purple of its eyes seared him within, and the pain smothered him. Nayu bowed his head and waited for death.

The pain waned.

"You deserve a slayer's death," the Siyeen said. "But I shall give you life, because you spoke the truth to your own hurt, when you could have held your peace. Go your way and be free of your guilt, for I have forgiven you."

Nayu could hardly believe the Siyeen's words, but, as he turned away toward his boat, he found that his feet would not go. He turned back.

"Permit me," he said. "You have granted me my life and forgiven my offense. Let me stay with you, so that you may not die alone."

"You may stay," said the Siyeen.

For three days, not speaking, not eating, only drinking the nearby waters to assuage his thirst, Nayu remained with the Siyeen and kept the flies and the watchful vultures away from the dying creature. At last, at the moonrise of the third day, the Siyeen's breath rattled and Nayu knew with the instinct of all living creatures that death hovered nearby.

"Child of man," the Siyeen said.

"I am here."

"Because you have stayed with me and showed kindness, I will show you a kindness also."

"I do not deserve it."

"Mercy is never deserved. That is why it is mercy. Come before me and look into my eyes."

Nayu came, and the purple eyes held him with such power that he could not look away, even if he wished to.

"I will give you the chance to live a second time. When you have reached this same mark in time, return to this place once more. Do not fail to do so."

"I will not fail."

The eyes of the Siyeen widened and consumed Nayu.

eight

the gift of the siyeen

When his consciousness returned to him, Nayu was a child again, roaming the waters of the marsh for his family's next meal, his mind small.

When the day came in which he had killed the young Siyeen, he removed his hand from his bow and watched the beautiful creature slide past him, carving the water into prisms and mirrors. It almost seemed as though the Siyeen knew his thoughts, for one wing-like fin rose from the waters, glittering, before the lithe body disappeared beneath the waters and Nayu saw him no more.

Years later, as a man, Nayu returned to the marsh island at the exact time that he had sworn to come. The old Siyeen lay in the shallows, dying, just as before, but nearby, the younger Siyeen awaited Nayu, a ripple of opalescent white in the shallows.

Nayu pulled his boat ashore and waded to the dying Siyeen.

"You are indeed a man of truth," the Siyeen said. "For you spoke the truth once to me, and you have also kept your word. For this, I will do you yet one more kindness."

"It is too much!" Nayu replied. "You spared my life when I deserved death, and you gave me the chance to erase my offense. What kindness do you owe me?"

"None," said the Siyeen, and Nayu thought he detected a smile in his voice. "But I will give it all the same."

The Siyeen labored for a breath, and at last continued. "The children of men are not lovers of truth. They are hard and self-serving. Even those who desire goodness fall utterly short of it, committing bitter deeds in their ignorance."

Nayu thought of his deadly arrow in the side of the young Siyeen, and nodded. "It is true. Our best efforts at goodness fail."

"The children of men wear human faces, but their hearts wear many shapes, the shapes of brutish creatures and weak beings. But the Siyeen must always wear the shape of its heart upon its body. You see me now as a winged eel, but I could look like a man, or a four-footed creature of the forest—whatever shape is truest to my heart at that moment. If angry, I am a fearsome beast. If grieving, I am wounded shadow. If happy, I am a creature of the air, scattering light to all. And where the Siyeen lives, the children of men are never without hope, for the Siyeen brings truth to them. As you stayed with me in my death, the Siyeen stays with the children of men in the living death of their corruption, that, though they do not know of its presence, they will never be utterly alone."

The Siyeen stirred and lifted its wing to brush Nayu's cheek. It felt like the touch of a loved one, and brought tears to his eyes.

"Because of my love for you," the Siyeen said. "I will give you my son. He will be your guardian and will teach you the ways of the Siyeen, the way of truth. You will learn how to see the hidden faces of the hearts of men. Seek truth always, and the truth will preserve you."

Nayu had no words and pressed his hand upon the side of the Siyeen, his head bowed, and felt the breath of the creature within it. At the moonrise, the old Siyeen released a long breath, then breathed no more. A soft light crept around the body of the Siyeen, like a mist, and when it cleared away, the body was no more.

When Nayu turned to go, he saw that a young man, about his age, waited by his boat. He recognized the purple eyes of the young Siyeen.

"Come," said the Siyeen.

Nayu followed the Siyeen, and began to learn the ways of the Siyeen. The years passed, and Nayu was enlightened like no other man before him, tempering justice with mercy, speaking with wisdom, and seeking truth always. The Siyeen never left his company, and traveled with him wherever he went, guarding his life from dangers and filling his heart with the light of true knowledge. They became like brothers. They slept under the same stars, ate the same food, drank the same waters, fought the same wars, and served the same people. There was no part of Nayu's life that lacked the influence and presence of the Siyeen, and thus he flourished.

One day, Nayu fell ill. It was a deadly illness that had claimed many of the People of the River, and his skin became pale and brittle like an onion's, and his eyes seemed to see only the pain inside him. He wrestled against death in the long watches of the night, but morning brought no relief. The Siyeen waited by him, in the familiar form of a man, as Nayu descended toward death.

At last, the Siyeen spoke.

"I have guarded and guided you thus far," he said. "I will not desert you in death. Cut open my side, brother, and you will see what a Siyeen can do."

At first, Nayu refused, but when the Siyeen insisted, he took up a knife and plunged it into the Siyeen's side. As the purple blood of the Siyeen flowed over Nayu's hands and body, the Siyeen turned his flashing eyes upon his friend and said gently, "A Siyeen's life may be given to whom he chooses. I choose you, Nayu. You will live because of me. Seek truth always, and the truth will preserve you."

"No, my brother!" Nayu, horrified, dropped the knife. "No. I do not want it."

"I give it freely," said the Siyeen. "And it is yours to give to another if you wish it. So it has always been. Whether by gift or by appointed birth, there will always be a Siyeen upon the earth, to carry the truth that preserves the lives of men."

As the blood poured over Nayu, he felt life return to him. The Siyeen absorbed Nayu's pain and sickness, and Nayu stayed and wept over his friend and brother until the light in the purple eyes died. When the soft light came to claim the body of the Siyeen, Nayu rose up from his knees. He was now the Siyeen and his dark eyes had transformed to purple.

Nayu married a woman who likewise loved truth, and became the father of many children. His sons became chieftains and his daughters became wise women, and from them came the clans of the People of the River. The Sarudi came from the eldest of Nayu's sons and the Karagi lived in the delta where Nayu had slain the Siyeen in his first boyhood.

When he was old and full of days, Nayu traveled into the marshlands and was never seen again. Some believe that he still lives, for the Siyeen lives a very long time, many lives of men. They say that he takes the form of a winged eel, and that, if you see his wings beneath the water, he will give you a second chance to live, in honor of the old Siyeen's gift to him.

The wise woman's gaze upon me is soft, and I realize that she ceased speaking many minutes ago, and I have stared into the fire, turning over thoughts in my mind like a bear turns over stones in the forest.

"Can the Siyeen see the future?" I ask, my voice husky.

"He sees men and women as they are and, sometimes, as they soon may be. The truth is never hidden from the Siyeen."

"Is the Siyeen ever born among people?"

"Yes. It is rare, but the old stories say it happens at times of great turbulence, when the clans forget the ways of truth. The Siyeen places its own offspring among the children of men, where the child lives as a man until its time."

"Its time?"

"The Siyeen is patient and its powers never emerge until there is need. Therefore it lives as a man, marked only by its eyes, until the time is ripe for its purpose to be fulfilled. Thus it is custom among the Sarudi to commit a purple-eyed child to the river. They call it the cursed child."

"If it is a creature of truth, why do they fear it?"

The wise woman is quiet for a few moments, then says, "A Siyeen is very dangerous."

Her tone chills my flesh, and I wait for her to continue. At last, she looks straight into my purple eyes, something that few people but

Uraun dare to do. "Tell me, Risha, what does truth do to a lie?"

My voice trembles. "It destroys it."

"If the children of men are, by nature, liars, who conceal their true faces, what shall the face of truth do to them but destroy them?"

I can hardly ask my next question. "Would the Siyeen destroy one it loves?"

The wise woman is silent for so long that I fear she will not answer.

"The Siyeen," she says at last, "does not destroy by design. Where it finds a lie, it acts because it cannot help it, as the light cannot help but fill the darkness."

I tremble again, and it seems that I am transparent before her.

"I am not the Siyeen," she says softly. "But I am descended from a daughter of Nayu, and can see the truth of some things. I will tell you what must be—and also what *may* be."

What we speak of next fills me with the heaviness of dread and sorrow. I do not tell her what I plan to do, but I suspect she knows.

When evening comes, I return to my boat, and she watches as I push it into the waters. I wade up to my knees, then swiftly leap over the side, settle myself, and raise my paddle. She stands still, watching my retreat, until the evening mists swallow her and I see her no more.

I turn away from the distant firelight of the village and set my course toward the marshes. I will be an exile before I will endanger my brother.

All night long, I lay in the bottom of my boat, feeling the roll of the waters beneath my shoulders and hips, blurring the sight of the cold, distant stars with my tears. When I raise my hand to wipe my cheeks, my fingers are dark and transparent, like a shadow. I feel like a shadow— a half-man, a formless being, a shade of grief— and somehow the sight of myself in this form is both repulsive and comforting. I know what I am, and I know that I have made the right choice.

Uraun seeks me. His boat arrives with the morning light, as the mists curl from the glassy waters. Abandoning his boat, he continues on foot in the shallows, wading through the marshes, calling my name until his voice is hoarse.

"Risha! I spoke to the wise woman. I know what you are. Do not fear me, Risha. I will not tell anyone. You are my brother. Come home."

His persistence nearly breaks my will, but I remain silent and hidden, weeping. At last he goes, and I cry until I fall into a stupor.

If only he knew. I am not afraid of him. I am afraid of myself, and what I may do to him.

NINE

The Protector

"Risha!" Uraun's voice cracks on my name. "By the River, Risha, I will not cease coming until I can speak to you face to face. Do you hear me? I will continue to come until you answer me."

I know Uraun's persistence. Can I risk it? If I do not, he will find me when I am not ready and I may do him more harm then than I would if I am prepared and resolute.

"Risha!" Uraun calls again.

"I am here!" The marsh seems to swallow my voice, but my brother's head snap toward the place where I wait amongst the marsh grasses. "Wait and I will come to you."

Uraun seats himself on the twisted branch of a marsh tree, drifting his feet in the water, as I paddled my small canoe through the deeper waters toward my brother. As soon as he sees me, his expression smooths and a quick grin flashes white across his dark-skinned face.

I almost feel that my decision has been unnecessary, evil even. Then I glimpse his reflection and see there the hideous fusion of my brother and the beast, and my purpose resolves. Uraun waits until I step onto the island of marshy ground by him and seat myself on another branch of the same tree. We are quiet for some time, our silence broken by the cries of the terns and the thrum from the wings of insects.

At last, Uraun speaks.

"So we have a name for what you are. A Siyeen. It is a gift, Risha."

I turn my face away and swallow hard.

"I spoke to the wise woman," Uraun says. "She told me all."

I doubt that. If she had, he would not be here.

"Come home, Risha. No one need know save me. We are brothers still, as much as if we share the same blood, and brothers should remain together."

"The beast remains with you, Uraun, and as long as it does, I cannot come home."

Uraun strikes the branch with sudden fury.

"I have not changed, nor is my heart any different than it has always been. What is this beast between you and I? I will not harm you, I swear it, and this beast you see shall not trouble you."

"You do not understand. A Siyeen is death to such a beast."

Uraun glances sharply at me. "The Siyeen is a creature of truth."

"And the beast is a creature of deception. I could kill you, Uraun."

Uraun laughs outright. "You? Save in the water, my skill is far greater than yours, Risha. I could kill you twice before you could kill me once."

"You saw what I did to the Sarudi."

"The Sarudi are children."

I stare at my brother. It has been eight days since our encounter with the Sarudi and he has already forgotten. It is foolish to hold your enemy's skill in contempt because you hate him, and yet more foolish to dismiss your brother's threat because you love him.

"Uraun, the Siyeen is a truth-protector. Wherever it sees a lie, it destroys it."

"Do you say I am a liar?"

I throw up my hands. There is no talking to my brother when he has sealed his mind upon something.

Uraun presses. "Do you say that you are the only defender of truth?"

Is this what the deception does to the truth: it twists it into the enemy? Every time I open my mouth, the truth becomes a blade against itself and Uraun retreats further and further into the deafness and blindness of the beast.

"Uraun, I will not return."

"Risha, this is madness! Think of what you are doing."

When Uraun is like this, no reason will persuade and my only strength lies in adamance. I remain silent while Uraun boils from earnestness to a blooded rage that sends echoes of fury across the waters.

"You are a fool!" Uraun snarls at last. "Perhaps it is better to be rid of your foolishness."

He does not look back when he strides away through the waters, but I watch him until he melts into the watercolor gray of the marshes. The bitterness in my throat squeezes my breath. This is not how I wish to part with my brother.

Yet there is a portion of my heart that is glad for his fury, for it, more than his persuasion, has confirmed my choice.

Uraun comes the next day and the next. At first, his anger burns and his words are bitter with my betrayal, with curses against my arrogance and repeated accusations of my foolishness. I do not answer him. There are some truths more potent in their silence, when the lie echoes into the darkness and its own returning sound is hollow and weightless.

Gradually, his anger subsides and one day he comes, seats himself at the twisted tree where we had met before, and says not a word. Then his head sinks into his hands and he remains, face hidden. His reflection, for once, is the same as the reality: a young man weeping.

Uraun's grief is far more difficult for me to bear than his anger. His anger reminds me of my purpose and the necessity of removing myself from him, but his grief is like blades in my chest and makes me wonder if perhaps I have judged him wrongly, if perhaps the beast is at last loosening its hold upon him.

But it is not so. I watch the reflections as a hawk watches the fish from above, and when Uraun's tears are dry, the beast returns.

Even so, I cannot abandon my brother completely.

"Risha," he says upon the twelfth day of my exile. "I know you will not return home. Perhaps you will not speak to me, but I know that you listen. You always were the better listener. I will come and speak and if you wish to listen, I will be glad to know that we remain brothers in that way. Will you do me at least this kindness: Will you give me tokens that you are well? I have no way of knowing if you are living or dead, if you have starved to death or been overtaken by disease or harmed by some wild animal. I cannot sleep if I fear for your life. Please, Risha. Please."

His voice breaks on the last word and I grit my teeth against the sight of my brother, slumped against the tree, his tears flowing between his fingers. When he is gone, I bring a basket I have woven of the thick grasses, filled with herbs and tubers, and set it in the crook of the tree.

Thus we begin an exchange. When Uraun comes, he brings tools and iron weapons traded from inland tribes—things I cannot make on my own—and I return them with feathers for his arrows and with valuables that the waters carry to me from the villages upriver.

Then Uraun speaks and I listen in hiding to his tales of his continuing training as a warrior, of the Sarudi encroachments upon the other People of the River, of the Karagi efforts to fortify and form alliances against their powerful enemy.

Life falls into a pattern. I live on a small island deep in the marshes and weave myself a dome-shaped hut, daubing it with clay to seal it. I hunt for whatever game the marshlands provide, and I fish often. I spend most days hunting and fishing from my boat, or fletching new arrows and roasting tubers on my island.

I am lonely, with a loneliness like pain. On moonlit nights, the sharper eyes among the Karagi see my new form: a weeping water-beast, with long, drooping whiskers and large, grieved eyes that swallow light. Some say that all who hear my wail must cry without knowing the reason.

Yet, for that first few years, I have the companionship of the wise woman, who knows me in any form by which I appear. I cannot visit often, lest Uraun or one of my cousins may seek me at her home. Her friendship is one of my few comforts.

I come to her one night in my nineteenth year in the form of an old man, sick with grief and loneliness. She looks into my dim and watering eyes, grasps my withered hand, and brings me into the scented shadows of her hut. There she brews me tea and lays me upon her bed and covers me with her own blanket.

"Are you certain this is the life you should choose?" she asks. "Uraun needs his brother."

"Not a brother who might kill him," the voice of the old man replies. "The creature on his back wants blood. But how much blood will satisfy? How long can I watch him become the creature? How long before the creature that I am can no longer suffer the blood-creature to pursue its aim?"

She nods and her hand cradles my cheek gently. It is this that I have missed—the innocent touch of skin to skin, the connection of gaze, the closeness of a soul. The marshes are desperately lonely and the need for companionship is like a thirst that drives the mind mad.

For a moment, she holds my gaze in her own, as though reading my soul through my eyes. Then she kisses my forehead and, before she turns away, I recognized the shine of tears upon her weathered cheeks.

When I wake the next morning, I am a boy again and I let her care for me, as though she is the mother that I lost. Neither of us speak much, but we do not need to.

Before evening comes, I leave her island for my own island.

In the cold season, a sickness sweeps through the Karagi and takes the wise woman. The Karagi cast her adrift in a burning boat to commit her body to the waters. I watch from afar, and feel that I have lost another mother.

TEN

SEEKING TRUTH

Uraun has not come today and the marshland delta has begun to receive dead that the survivors were not able to recover from the swifter waters.

I find my cousin, barely twenty summers old, one who had always treated me kindly despite my purple eyes. His body is swollen with water and pale from the loss of blood from the vicious tear in his side. I speak a prayer over his body, committing his soul to the rest of the afterlife.

It is the least service I can do for my people, to return the lost dead. My small boat is burdened with the Karagi when I set out by the light of a slivered moon.

I enter the water and the change begins almost immediately, a shiver like the ripple of wind over the hairs of my body. A Siyeen's gift is to become what it most feels at the moment, and in the water I feel like one with the currents. Thus I become a transparent being, as though water had coalesced into a man. In this way, disguised, I travel to the hidden tributary where I know Uraun still lays his fish-traps below the water and, cloaked in the darkness brought by concealing clouds, I lay the dead in respectful repose along the shore and light a fire around their bodies to keep away scavengers until the Karagi can discover their dead.

The next day, Uraun arrives, his lip swollen and his face so pale that the scar upon his cheek is nearly invisible. It is clear that his appointment with me has cost him a great deal of his strength, but he is Uraun—what he determines to do, he does.

For a time, he slumps upon the tree branch, his head bowed with exhaustion. At last, in a voice hoarse with the shout of the battle, he speaks.

"We met the Sarudi at the place of the White Stone, within the territory they have lately taken from the Andani, our allies. The battle was fierce. We lost so many, Risha, so many good men. The battle ranged for miles and the forest burned around us and the waters were choked with blood. I slaughtered them like beasts, Risha, until

I had no breath left in me and I could not unwrap my fingers from my knife. It is but a pale repayment for what they did to our father, what they continue to do to our people."

He pauses and spits to the side painfully.

"We were victorious, my brother, but at a price that is almost more than I can bear. We lost two cousins besides Hagur, whom you returned. Most grievous, we lost our uncle. He is gone, Risha."

From my hiding-place amongst the grasses, I fold upon myself in a spasm of grief, remembering the generosity of the man who had sheltered my mother and become my father without fear of my purple eyes.

"The chieftain also lies mortally wounded," Uraun continues, clearing the tears from his throat. "He is expected to die before the night is over and the elders have already assembled to discuss the matter of his successor, for his only son was taken during the sickness earlier this year. I will tell you their decision when I know."

He pauses, then adds, "Risha, I know that you fear what you are, what you represent to mankind. But I ask you to consider your people. What is a protector of truth if life is not preserved? Is it not significant that the first time your true nature was revealed, you were acting in defense of yourself and of me? Yet now you hide yourself and avoid those you love and who love you, and refuse to interfere even while the river runs with the blood of your kinsmen and the dead stink under the sky. You have the means, Risha, to preserve life. You fear that by acting you will endanger life, but I tell you that your inaction endangers life as well. If you were a mere man, you would take up the knife and the spear and the bow in defense of your people and your family. It makes no sense that, because you are more than a man, you do less than a man would do. Truth is more than an ideal, Risha, a puff of smoke in a gray sky. *Truth acts.* Truth cannot be truth unless it upholds life and loyalty and justice and mercy. If you cannot see this, Risha, you are no preserver of truth. You are only a coward."

My brother's words skewer my chest like ice and I remain still and shaken long after he has gone and the bitter echoes of his voice have fallen silent across the waters.

I have mistaken passivity for wisdom. How could someone who loves truth so deeply err so greatly?

I have failed as a man. I have failed as a Siyeen.

I abandon my boat and throw myself into the waters. Bitterly, I ask myself: What is the form of failure? I curve to catch a glimpse of my body, expecting to see my limbs overtaken by some hideous fungus or a black rot. But no, I am merely a man and my lungs burn for air.

Man. Man is the shape of failure. I have failed because I thought as a man and not as a Siyeen. But how would a Siyeen think?

A thought winks into existence like the first spark of a fire, spreading across my mind like molten gold.

I rise to the surface, gasp for air, and sense a quiet descend upon my troubled mind. Then I slip beneath the water and focus upon my object.

I am a Siyeen. I am a wearer of truth. I will seek the truth until I find its answer.

I am aware of time and water slipping past me as I swim through the deep waters of the marsh, aware of my rising to the surface for air and my return to the dimness of the waters, the warmth of my body's movement within the coolness of the marsh.

What is true? I will not rest until I know.

Suddenly my feet strike ground and I stumble into the shallows of a marshland island. Exhaustion drags my limbs and it requires all my strength to bear my own weight to the shore, where I collapse upon a tangle of stone and grass.

Gray mists gather like sleep around me, obscuring my vision, casting all forms into ghostly silhouettes, warping sounds so that even the sound of my own slowing breaths seems alien to me.

Strange visions enter into my mind. Am I dreaming?

The elders of the clan sit in a circle around the fire, the firelight chasing shadows across their sunken cheeks and lined foreheads. The Karagi wait around them, silent and marked on the heart, the lips, the forehead, mourning for the chieftain they have lost in battle. Uraun waits among the other warriors, his lip still swollen, but I am glad to see that color has returned to his face.

"We have considered carefully," an elder speaks. "We have chosen the next chieftain. It is he to whom we give the white stone."

The Karagi wait, breath suspended, as the elder rises to his feet, the white stone in the hollow of his palm like a glimmer of first light.

Then he turns Uraun's palm upright and places the stone within it.

Uraun stares, stricken, at the elder.

I know that my brother's heart is that of a leader and that he has never questioned his abilities, but at this moment, he looks more like the old Uraun I remember, the boy who just lost his father.

Then Uraun bows his head and kneels before the elder as the old man speaks with a voice that resonates to every ear.

"In battle, you are Courage. Among your people, you are Loyalty. In your words, you are Wisdom. Uraun, son of Tungat, you are a man of worth and shall be a chieftain of greatness. The Karagi honor you."

The people bow their heads and touch their fingertips to their hearts, their lips, their foreheads. "We honor you!"

Uraun swallows hard, then dips his head in acknowledgement of the people, his people.

In the reflection of his dark eyes, I see the blood-beast but I also see a boy.

My brother is not beyond redemption.

Now I see my error clearly. I have thought of truth as a fire that destroys the lie and all who are captured by it, like a wildfire that cannot distinguish between grass and creature. This is true, that all who shelter with the lie share in its eventual destruction, but there is more.

The truth is a refining fire, that destroys the rough ore until the impurities fall away and the metal runs like liquid, ready to be molded into the form that serves men best.

The truth destroys in order to save.

I have found my answer.

I wake without transition, rested and aware. As I sit upright, my shoulder brushes against a curving white staff ascending toward the sky. Turning, I observe that a double row of such staffs spread across the earth, half consumed by grasses and moss, curving inward as though bowing to one another. Beyond them, a smooth white boulder glimmers in the breaking dawn.

The prickle at the back of my neck spreads down my shoulders and shudders through my limbs.

These were no mere visions. I have dreamed within the skeleton of the ancient Siyeen who gifted Nayu with his son.

ELEVEN

JUSTICE AND MERCY

I leave Uraun a garland of willow and iris leaves, skillfully entwined according to the chieftain's pattern of the ancient river peoples. When Uraun sees it, he laughs aloud.

"You know that I am chieftain of the Karagi, then? You sly fish, Risha. I knew it! You have been spying on me and someday I will catch you at it and force you to come home."

He seems very pleased with this knowledge and I smile a little to myself at his expansive mood. It is good to see Uraun happy for once.

Then Uraun sobers.

"My skill as leader shall be tested very soon. We have heard that the Sarudi are attempting to claim the northern forest. If they do so, they will cut us off from the river and our livelihood. We will have to make a stand, but we have so few warriors. I have chosen the place. If we occupy the high ground and take them by surprise, we can drive them against the river. It is our only chance for so few to prevail against so many, but even the laying of the trap may cost many lives."

He pauses, then speaks through a hollow weariness, like a man with no blood inside his body. "It is a privilege to lead the Karagi warriors, Risha. I would be proud to die beside any one of them. But that is my fear—death unvictorious. My position as chieftain is a great honor and a grave burden. I fear to fail their bravery."

I have rarely heard my brother speak so honestly of his own limitations. He had never done so when I lived with him and I can hardly believe that, were I standing in front of him, he would speak so vulnerably. I wonder if he no longer remembers me as his brother, if he simply sees me as some invisible spirit of the marsh to whom he can speak, without response, the listener whose judgment he need not fear, whose counsel he need not seek. Am I still a man to my brother?

When Uraun leaves, I sit in silence for a long while. Time is slow here in the marshes, liquid and ever-renewing like the waters, without the haste and drive of the civilized life. I contemplate like one of the rainbow-winged dragonflies. At last, I reach a decision and rise to act with the swiftness of intention and instinct.

I feel no division about what I have determined to do, as a man would before battle— the mingling of fear and power. I feel only a colorless emotion, like the resolve of a creature that has only the immediate, immutable demands of life before it.

What I feel becomes my reality, and I recognize the soft tingling shudder, like cool rain on my skin as my legs fuse and my eyes drift to opposite sides of my elongating face. I am a river perch, and the spiny fin along my back carves the water as I battle upriver all night long to reach the northern forest. The river is swifter and narrower there, obstructed and eddied by rocks, and it takes all my strength as a man to clamber to the shore, naked and dripping. I cannot afford for the Sarudi to find me, so before the light emerges over the lip of the ravine, I thrust myself up the steep embankment, clawing for purchase on the spongey turf of old leaves and discarded pine needles. The rocks erupt from the landscape here, leaning upon one another to create hidden crevasses and caves. I take refuge in one, until my breath returns to me and the damp cold quivers in my bones.

I know how to wait.

Three Sarudi warriors pass within an arm's distance from my hiding place and do not see me. They speak as they continue and my keen hearing, honed through the quietness of the marsh, follows them as they go.

"The Karagi approach from the south," one tells the others, gesturing toward the invisible enemy. "But there is a small party sweeping from the east, to trap us against the river. They are weak when divided and we have the greater numbers. We will make our first stand there, on that ridge, then give before them, as though we will fall into their trap. When our first group descends the bank in this direction, then we shall raise up a larger party behind them, so that the Karagi themselves will be forced upon the river." He pauses, then adds grimly, "They should have accepted the peace we offered them. What is payment of a tribute when they now face the loss of all their warriors? The river has delivered them to us this day. Not one shall escape with his life."

The Sarudi begin to move with the suppressed coil of hunters, their weapons ready and their attention taut like a drawn bowstring. I know how silently the death of warriors comes, the whisper of arrows slicing the air, the pad of moccasined feet on soft earth, the sharp rustle of birds startled to flight. It is not in my heart to wait until the soundless battle has overtaken my kinsmen. I mark the Sarudi warriors by their shadows and the flickers of their movement amongst the rocks and trees. There are perhaps a hundred warriors to the Karagi's fifty.

But the Karagi will survive today.

Now is my moment.

All the People of the River know that blood calls for blood and the desecration of the dead is an insult worse than defeat. The Karagi deserve justice against the Sarudi. But peace is not won only with weapons. I will offer the Sarudi their lives.

I rise amidst my enemy, naked and weaponless, striding with purpose. Some shout to warn their brethren and I pause, anticipating an arrow in my ribs at any moment. But it does not come.

"Sarudi warriors!" I call. "This is an unjust war. The Karagi have not wronged you. Your lands are not too bare to support you. The dead are no threat to you and yet you mutilate them. You are swollen with pride and bloated with greed. The Karagi have fought honorably and you yet you lie in wait for their warriors. But I tell you that you yourselves are in danger, for thought you cannot see it, there are more with them than with you. Turn back, while you have your lives, and seek peace."

Only a derisive laugh answers me. "Who are you, O bare-buttocked youth, to speak to elders and seasoned warriors that way? Stay here and watch how we deal with impudence."

"Stay!" calls a voice, and I recognize Kaheela, the same man who urged caution when Uraun and I were captured by the Sarudi as boys. "Shanak, beware his eyes!"

But Shanak snorts. "Curse or no curse, I will not suffer this youth to speak so to the Sarudi, nor to remain alive to tell his kinsmen of our position."

"Shanak...!"

I move by instinct and the arrow hisses into the forest behind me. Heat climbs from my chest to my face, and my stomach burns. He does not fear the truth-wearer? He seeks innocent blood? Then he shall learn.

The ones who strike at me or seek my harm, I mow like grass before a scythe, and forty of their warriors fall wasted by fire and claw before me. The ones who flee, I pursue as far as the waters of the river, where I watch them splash like children in their panic.

There is one who does neither. Kaheela kneels on the same place where I had addressed the Sarudi, unmoving, head bowed. When I approach from the river, having melted back into the form of a man, he lifts his face to me, the heaviness of death in his eyes.

For a long time, he and I regard one another in silence. Then I speak sharply.

"Why did you not run when I pursued your kinsmen to the river?"

The lump in his throat dips as he swallows. "Because you cannot outrun a Siyeen."

"Why do you stay?"

"Because perhaps my contrition will earn me mercy."

"You demand mercy?"

"It is not mine to demand. I only ask it."

I observe Kaheela closely. An honorable Sarudi warrior? We would see.

"Come here!" I beckon darkly. "Follow me to the river."

He still carries his weapons and I half-expect a knife in my back, but we reach the river without incident.

"Kneel by the water."

Kaheela draws in a long breath but does not tremble as he lays aside his bow and slowly sinks to the earth, where the river laps at his bent knees. The surface of the water ripples and twists, but I only need a glimpse.

There.

In life, he is nearly fifty years old, but in his reflection, he is white-haired as a man thirty years older, yet the grip and sinew of his arms remains unabated.

The stirring in my chest surprises me, but I welcome it also. There is an understanding of nobility between warriors, too sacred to ignore.

"Rise, Kaheela."

He glances at me, astonished, and I gesture to confirm my command.

"You are wiser than your people, Kaheela, and you are not so very far from the truth. I have spared your life twice. I will not spare it a third time. If you ever lift your hand against the Karagi again, I will slay you."

Kaheela nods, his jaw clenched. With my right thumb, I touch his bare chest at his heart, then his lips and his forehead.

"Seek truth always and the truth will preserve you."

Where my thumb touches, the skin turns white like a scar—the mark of my warning and my protection upon him. I did not know I had the power to create a mark of permanence, but what is more indelible than the truth?

I turn and stride away, but his voice recalls me.

"Siyeen!"

I twist to look upon him and he smiles a little.

"Do you know what the Sarudi say of the Siyeen and why he who bears the purple eyes is considered a cursed child?"

"No."

"The truth is the weapon of justice, thus the Sarudi deem the truth-wearer to be a curse, because men are not just and therefore the truth-wearer becomes their bane. They kill such children among the Sarudi, before they can bring justice to the deeds of men."

"Then the Sarudi are twice accursed for the blood of the innocent."

"Yes," said Kaheela, his cheeks flushing with shame. "But you have taught me more this day."

More? I wait, intrigued.

"You have taught me that truth can become mercy as well, that the same power that wields a weapon against darkness and deception also protects and forgives. The Sarudi have forgotten this about the Siyeen and they fear what they should love. Justice without mercy is a terrible thing; who can stand before it and where may redemption be found? Mercy without justice is a terrible thing; where shall order be sought and wickedness find an end to its plunders? Thus, the Siyeen is most itself when it is both avenger and healer."

I cannot answer, but his words slay me as surely as if he has driven a blade through my heart. I twist on my feet and hasten away, lest he should see my tears and know that the truth-wearer is not only a creature of power, but also a man and thus capable of weeping.

TWELVE

WHISPERS

The Sarudi attempt twice more to overcome the Karagi, but each time, through the knowledge of the dreams amongst the Siyeen bones, I thwart their destruction of my people.

Each time, I deliver a warning to them, the same that I gave before my destruction of them in the northern forest.

On the first attempt, the Sarudi shoot to kill, but I have positioned myself on the high ground, with an escape route that they will struggle to duplicate, for my years as an exile has gifted me with the craft of the wild creatures.

I kill many Sarudi that day, but spare those who flee.

On the second attempt, the Sarudi slide down the river in their slender canoes, under cover of a moonless night. When I speak my warning, the Sarudi do not even resist. Opposition with me would be foolishness, for they can see only with men's eyes in the dark, but I could see with the eyes of a Siyeen and a dweller of the wild. They know this and simply turn their boats in the river, returning silently to the place from whence they have come.

The Sarudi do not come again nor do they lie in wait for the Karagi.

"I know it was you," Uraun says, when he comes to the marsh. "My scouts are not too few to mark the Sarudi slain by a great wild animal in the very places where they lay in wait for us, nor to overlook the stories that travel throughout the People of the River of the white beast with burning purple eyes that does not suffer the dishonorable to live. You have done well, Risha, and for that you have earned my deepest gratitude."

I do not know if I have done well, but I have adhered to the truth as best I know. I wonder what Nayu would have done and if he still roams the marshes where I walk and swim. If only I could ask him, to know what the spirit of a true Siyeen would say.

A tense peace binds the People of the River and I journey to the Siyeen island often to gain knowledge of any threat to my people, but either there are no such threats or the Siyeen dreams do not show them. But perhaps it is not good for a truth-wearer to have the answer always given and rarely sought. Therefore, I begin long forays into the territories of the clans of the People of the River, watching the movements of the warriors; observing their sowing, their hunting, their reaping; learning their ways and their lands; always returning in time for Uraun's visits, lest I should miss important news.

One day, as Uraun speaks at the gnarled tree, some unfamiliarity jars my eyes and, looking closer at my brother's reflection, I see something behind him, as though smoke and shadow have congealed into the shape of a man who stoops and whispers in his ear.

Who is my brother's counsel?

The next day, I take the form of a fish—it is the form truest to me when I am in the water— and wind against the current to the Karagi village at the bend of the river. There are few Karagi men, for only my efforts spared the last of the warriors from utter destruction, and many old and sick. When Uraun strides through the camp, the growing boys flock to his side and he smiles a little, though he does not break stride. An old woman nods at him in respect and he returns a short nod of acknowledgement. Women hustle their toddlers out of his way, whispering that Chief Uraun has many duties and should not be disturbed. There is not a warrior who looks upon Uraun with anything less than the deepest respect, even the older warriors who trained my brother and I when we were boys.

Uraun is chief not only in name but in actuality, and my greatest wish is that the man he becomes in his reflection is as noble as the man that his people see in him.

For the next several weeks, I look for signs that he has an advisor who may wish him harm, but I can see none. He has a multitude of counselors, warriors of both age and repute, to whom he gives great honor, and all of them appear to have only Uraun's and the Karagi interest in their counsel. They accompany Uraun in his dealings with neighboring clans, including the Sarudi, and in his hunting expeditions.

I am patient and, one by one, I catch glimpses of the counselors' reflections. Some have burdens upon their backs to represent their troubles, some are straight and powerful, some have faces in the back of their heads to indicate their wary nature, some are men of blood but their weapons are turned away from Uraun toward the other clans.

A very few have the same youthful and light-filled expressions as the wise woman had possessed during her life.

The danger must not be from the Karagi. But from where would it come then?

Some days after I have concluded my investigations and remain mulling over the results, Uraun arrives at the meeting branch, seats himself, and is quiet a long time before he speaks.

"Since you wasted the Sarudi, their clan has offered peace talks to the Karagi. I have attended many meetings with them, both in my village and theirs, to come to an arrangement. They may have greater numbers, but they dare not lift their hand against us and the wrath of the Karagi will be fierce against them if they should try."

The wrath of the Karagi would be useless against the Sarudi, but I hold my tongue.

"The Sarudi request access to the fishing waters of the delta, which they would have had in friendship for a small recompense if they had only respected the Karagi instead of declaring war on us and slaying like beasts. I have forced them to pay a high tribute for safe passage through our waters and for continued peace between our people. I will grind the Sarudi into the very dust that they kicked in our peoples' eyes. They will pay for all the evil that they have sown and all the deaths they have caused."

I almost break my vow of exile to myself and spring into Uraun's presence to throttle him. Uraun! This is not what I protected the Karagi for. You are making the Karagi like the Sarudi.

But if I reveal myself when I am angry, when his reflection shows a man so warped by the hunger for power and vengeance, I may at last do what I have feared I will do; I may destroy my brother in destroying the lie that lives inside him.

"As part of the peace," Uraun continues, unknowingly, "I have demanded the chieftain's daughter as my bride. Her father will never attack the Karagi while she is mine. She is surety that my people shall be safe for the duration of her lifetime which, as she is hearty and well-pleasing to look upon, should be for many years yet. I have also required a percentage of the young boys to be trained as Karagi warriors."

How can love for one's people become so entangled with the self's desires?

When Uraun departs, I paddle my boat furiously through the deep waters of the marshes, then peel off my clothing, abandon my boat, and swim until exhaustion numbs my anger.

Can the truth be silent when the lie has taken root? If it was wrong to remain passive when action was required, would it not also be wrong to remain silent when my brother must be warned?

I return to my boat, pull my clothing back onto my wet body, and make plans.

I wait in one of the tributaries until a boy of about eight years of age comes to check his fish traps in the evening. He lifts the trap from the water, removes the two fish and slaps them against a rock until they quiver no more, then threads them with a supple branch to carry them home for the family's pot.

As he turns to go, I rise from my hiding place. He remains frozen where he stands and the color drains from his face.

"Do you know who I am?" I ask quietly.

He nods.

"Will you bring a message to your chief from me? Be certain that only his ears will hear it."

He nods again.

"I have watched you, Onak. You are bright, obedient, and you have a good memory. My message must be delivered word for word. Do you understand?"

"Yes, Siyeen."

I wish he would call me Risha. Even a Siyeen desires a name.

"Tell Uraun this: I did not protect the Karagi from annihilation so that they might expand their reach over the clans. Let victory be enough and do not stripe your enemy's cheeks when he dares not retaliate. You will not use me as a weapon against the Sarudi. If you choose to exert control over another clan, your own warriors can bear the price of your vengeance; I will have no part in it. But consider, Uraun. When justice has been served, it is the warrior's honor to extend mercy. Let the clans say that Uraun of the Karagi is mighty in war and magnanimous in peace."

I make Onak repeat the message until it is as marked upon his memory as it is on mine.

"Go now," I say. "Your family will be awaiting you."

The boy lingers for a moment, then, almost embarrassed, he offers me the two fish in both hands.

"I have no need of them," I say. "Keep them for your family."

"No, but you are the Siyeen and the brother of my chieftain. Please take my fish."

The gifts given from such simplicity of kindness should not be refused. I accept the two fish and watch as the boy clambers up the embankment toward the glimmer of gold light that fans the sky with luminance from just beyond the brow of the hill.

The next day, Uraun arrives at the meeting place in a foul mood.

"Tell me, Risha, how much blood did you spend on victory? Show me your scars! My warriors and I have fought like men—yes, and with the mortality and vulnerability of men—against a foe much more numerous than us, and you see fit to send a child to warn me of growing power-hungry? For the last few years, as you have imitated the frogs and flitted with the birds, I could not breathe without fear of choking on an arrow, or go to the woods to relieve myself without fear of being slain, or live a single day without news of some dire threat to my people. And you wish me to withdraw my advantage from the Sarudi? I do not hear your voice for years and receive no word from you, and your first message to me is to beware of taking the necessary measures to ensure the future prosperity of my people? By the waters, you call yourself a truth-wearer and yet you wear only cowardice and meddling and contention! I will have none of it. Do you hear? None of it!"

I am glad that Uraun leaves so quickly, for I can hardly breathe for the wrath boiling in my chest. Uraun has forgotten in whose strength he achieved victory. I ask for no credit, but I will not have my protection used as a weapon to humiliate a clan and destroy its sovereignty. It is not done among the People of the River.

After a time, my anger cools and in its place, I feel a deep despondency. What whispers are my brother listening to? How can I find the one who fills Uraun with an insatiable hunger for more?

Thirteen

URAUN'S BRIDE

I journey to the Sarudi village by the river, traversing the waters in the form of an eel, though not a winged one. I have never taken that form, the truest form of the Siyeen, and I am afraid of what it might mean if I should find myself in that shape.

From beneath the sheen of the rippling surface, I watch the Sarudi women for several days until I learn which one is the chieftain's daughter. She is not a beautiful woman, but she possesses a modest kind of attractiveness that I think may suit my brother well.

I reserve my judgment of her until she comes to the river to bathe and I can observe her reflection. Although her body is strong, the wavering image on the water's surface shows a thin, frail creature—one without weight or will of her own—and behind her, a dark shadow who presses a blade into her fist and guides her arm.

It is the same shadow that has whispered to my brother's reflection for the last several months.

The threat is Sarudi.

I return to the marshlands and wait for Uraun's return. I wish the People of the River knew the art of reading and writing, for then I would not be forced to speak to him face to face. If I approach him, I shall wear the face of his brother, for in his presence, it is the truest image I could bear. I tremble, fearing that the necessity of our meeting will yet betray my brother, but I determine that I will stay at a distance from him, and let the stillness of the marsh carry my voice to him.

Uraun deserves at least this much. One thing at least he spoke that was true: If I must speak with him, I should do it face to face and not by substitute. The truth should not hide.

If I destroy my brother, the grief of my deed would destroy me, but it is a risk I must take, or I risk losing him through my distance and allowing him to become a bringer of death.

But Uraun does not come, and when, some nights later, the sounds of singing and celebration ripple over the waters, I know I am too late. I wrestle in the dark with myself, and my reflection shows a wrinkled, weeping child. It disgusts me, and I close my eyes to it.

Uraun comes no longer to the marshlands and I do not go to him.

He has chosen his way. I will watch for the subtleties of the shade's whisper to make itself manifest and do what I can to protect him, even if he never acknowledges or knows of my action on his behalf. But I cannot live his life for him.

If only he could begin his life again.

When I journey to the village by night, shaped as an eel, Uraun stands at the edge of the river as he has done since childhood, as though awaiting our father's return. When I see my brother, my sinuous body parts and hardens, and I know I am a man again. I am more accustomed now to the suddenness of my transformations, as my emotions shift and thoughts change. I remain amidst the reeds, my face just above the river's surface.

Uraun looks inscrutable in the moonlight, his face like stone, but I can read his heart with one glance at his reflection, and what I see chills me. His reflection gazes directly at my face, and on his back, the frail chieftain's daughter clings around his neck and whispers words into his ear, as she hears them from the shadow who stands behind her. As I watch, the reflected Uraun brings up his arm, and I sense, rather than see, the arrow release toward me. I flinch away, blurring the reflection with my movement. On the bank, Uraun snaps from his reverie and his eyes pierce through the darkness, seeking me, but I slip beneath the waters and flash away, becoming an eel again as I retreat.

Something is wrong. What does the shadow speak to Uraun through the Sarudi chieftain's daughter? Why should it mean danger to *me*?

I dare not speak directly to Uraun, but I can speak to another.

She sits upon a fallen log, her seat cushioned with moss and her black hair braided down her back. Her basket of herbs rests upon the tangle of moldering leaves and rocky earth at her feet. She closes her eyes and lifts her face heavenward, and the light spangles upon her copper skin as she remains still for several breaths.

I emerge from my hiding place, lean against a tree trunk, fold my arms across my chest, and wait silently.

She opens her eyes.

She does not move, but it is as though the breath freezes in her throat. Then, slowly, she falls from her seat to her knees, her eyes filling with tears, her chin trembling.

"Please."

Her terror spears me. I stride forward with the soft-footedness of a deer and crouch to clasp her hands in mine.

"Huntara, do not fear. I am not here to harm you."

"What are you here for then?" she asks, tears still uncoiling down her cheeks. I wipe them away, embarrassed that the mere sight of me should be cause for such distress. Am I so much a monster?

"I only wish to speak to you," I say. "May I sit with you?"

She nods, but it is the acquiescence of one who dares not refuse. I help her regain her seat on the log and seat myself next to her, still holding her hands, sensing the trembling of her limbs through them.

"I will not hurt you," I repeat and wait for several minutes as she regains her courage and breath. At last, when she is sufficiently recovered, she avoids my gaze and asks, "Why are you here?"

"I wish to know how my brother fares and how you fare. Tell me, are you happy with Uraun?"

She glances sharply at me. She knows she cannot lie to a Siyeen.

"Have no fear, Huntara. An honest answer means more to me than a pleasing one. I only wish to know…"

I sigh and glance away through the forest, at the striping of light and shadow and the myriad of greens. So many shades of green, like the tangle of emotions in a human breast. Even the truth can be complicated at times.

"Uraun is very gentle with me," Huntara says. "And very kind. He is stern and cold with my father, and harsh with my people, but he has always treated me with dignity. I still fear him, but…"

She pauses and blushes deeply. I know the meaning of that color in the face of a woman and the shine of her black eyes.

"You are fond of him then?"

Huntara hesitates, then nods briefly, almost as though she is afraid of the admission.

"He is different among the Karagi than when he is among the Sarudi. I see now why his people love him."

"Do you think he is happy?"

"Happy?" She frowns. "He is pleased that peace is achievable between our people now and that the trade agreements are moving forward. He loves his people and his ability to serve and guide them as chieftain. In his own way, I believe he has affection for me."

She looks at me mutely, as though asking me to understand what she does not know how to say.

I understand. I know Uraun too well.

"He is stern with the Sarudi," I say. "What do the Sarudi feel about him?"

Tears well into her eyes again and her trembling returns. "What can I say? My people know that you are his brother and that you will waste anyone who offers harm to Uraun. They have no defense left, Siyeen. They must make peace with Uraun or risk slaughter."

I want to tell Huntara that I would never indiscriminately kill her people, that there were limitations to my protection, but clearly Uraun has never told anyone of my warning to him. There are dangers to making known my thoughts. Silence is prudent for Uraun's sake, even though he perpetuates the misperception of my loyalties. I wish that I had some means to reassure the oppressed Sarudi that I am not like my brother, but I bite my tongue.

"Do you see your people often?"

"I meet with my father sometimes when they come to the Karagi village and, if Uraun permits me, I accompany Uraun to the Sarudi village and meet with the Sarudi women."

"It is good that you can see your family."

I must have allowed more emotion in my voice than I meant to, for suddenly it is no longer I who am holding her hands for comfort, but she who clasps my fingers to communicate compassion.

"You miss him," she says with a peculiar ache in her voice. "You miss Uraun."

I cannot speak, and the pain in my throat throbs like a stone has lodged within it.

"Is there no one who cares for you?" Huntara asks softly.

I cannot bear her gentleness. It is like salt in an open wound and my emotions writhe against it. I rise with haste and wince back the tears that have arrived against my will.

"I am glad that Uraun has you as his bride," I say huskily.

"Are you?" She meets my eyes for the first time, holds them despite her peoples' fear of the purple eyes. There is some trouble within her gaze and the question is more than a desire for confirmation.

"What do you see in me, Siyeen?"

So I am Siyeen again and not Risha. The emotional distance helps me to recollect my scattered composure. Her eyes do not relent.

"I see a woman of compassion and insight," I reply. "You balance Uraun well."

"But what do you see in my reflection?"

For a long time, we gaze at one another, hardly daring to breathe. Then:

"I see a shade whispering in your ear and a knife in your hand. I see your will being shaped by the will of another."

A shudder passes down her body and her face drains of color.

"I wish no harm to your brother. Please believe me."

"I know the truth when I see it, Huntara. When I said that I was glad that you are Uraun's bride, I meant it. But if you know of any threat to him, you must tell me. For his sake as well as your peoples'."

The brief friendship between us flows away like water in a drying tributary. I have made her responsible for betraying her people in order to save them from the wrath of the Siyeen. That is not how I mean it, but I cannot tell her more.

I speak so little to anyone in my exile, but it seems that every time I open my mouth, I do the work of a divider and a fool.

I hate myself.

Huntara's expression blanks into a wide terror and the tingle in my body alerts me to the change. I turn, my hands hiding my face, but the claws of a beast have already sprouted from my fingertips. Whatever the shape of one who hates himself, it must be terrible to behold. I make no attempt to hide the noise of my passing as I drive myself deep into the forest, away from Huntara and the impossible conflict between our people.

FOURTEEN

The Two Faces of Huntara

Uraun comes to me in the marsh some days later, the first time that he has had attempted to contact me since his marriage five months previously. He does not storm or rage, but there is a blood-fire in his eyes that I know too well. Whatever I have done to offend him must be severe indeed.

"Risha!" My name bounces back to him from the water, the trees, the sky. "Is it not enough that peace is so hard won, but you must make a mockery of it also? I fought for peace, I negotiated for peace, and I married for peace. Now you cast all my efforts into doubt. I gave you no leave to do as you have done."

What does he talk about? If he feels I misspoke to his wife, he should at least do me the dignity of presenting a full accusation. These allusions and riddles perplex me.

"You do not fight for our people. You fight for yourself. Whatever your aim is, it is folly and injustice. Do not touch the Sarudi again, or I shall hunt you down."

The Sarudi? This is news that I cannot even begin to decipher.

As soon as Uraun is gone, his enraged and smoking reflection with him, I spring up from my hiding place and make my way as both man and beast to the Sarudi village, which sits on the high place upriver. I see the smoke before I even reach the place, and its color is blacker and its ascent thicker than should smoke from tame fires. The smell is acrid, a smell like burnt furs and skins. I know the smell of desolation.

The faces of the people are drawn as they go about their duties, tending the wounded, drawing water from the river to quench the flames. There is little they can do to clear the debris of the burnt huts and property until the heat subsides, and their faces bear the patience of suffering.

Uraun arrives nearly as soon as I do and gazes at the smoking wreckage of homes.

"I have spoken with the Siyeen," says Uraun.

The Sarudi chieftain's cheek twitches and he stammers, "Honorable chieftain, we do not wish to make any accusations." Of course he would not wish to slander the powerful brother of his victorious enemy. "We only know that all witnesses agree that the attack appeared to come from above, for there are no tracks, and it ended as quickly as it came. But three have died, burnt alive by the attacker, and much property is ruined. We do not know what to think, but we need assurance that you do not wish us harm. Though it may, perhaps, be heinous to certain people that a Sarudi woman has joined with a Karagi chieftain, we remain loyal to the truce we struck. We are in your hand, Uraun, and we have honored the peace between us."

"By the soul of my father, I never authorized such an attack nor wished it. The peace between us still stands. I have spoken to the Siyeen and I will ensure that this never happens again."

Do you know me so little, Uraun, that I am the first one you must blame for this? Do you love me so little that I no longer have a name to you?

I withdraw and consider the day's events.

If neither Uraun nor I did this murderous deed, who has dared to trouble the Sarudi? Have some of Uraun's men felt that his treatment of the Sarudi was too lenient for the crimes they committed against the Karagi? But such actions would conflict with the Karagi way, for their warriors are taught to stand and fight like men, with their face to the enemy and their backs to cowardice. Also, the manner of burning evidently led suspicion to fall upon me, and what Karagi would be foolish enough to make me seem an enemy to Uraun's people, when I had helped them to attain such victory over a more numerous adversary? But perhaps that is exactly the ruse that would give the most impunity to the secret assailants. No one could touch a Siyeen and make him pay for his crimes, so why not blame him? And who but Uraun would question a Siyeen's judgment?

I watch the reflections of the Karagi for several days and observe the same reflections that I did before. They have their faults, but they wish neither me nor my brother harm.

If the Karagi do not seek to ruin an already overcome people, who would?

I visit the other clans, but though I encounter both good men and bad, I cannot find evidence that they would attack the Sarudi. Who, then, is sowing such confusion amongst the Sarudi?

Perhaps it is time to dream as a Siyeen.

I have not been to the island in nearly a year, for I am careful of the time I spend there. Desire for knowledge of all things, of possible futures, becomes a trap for the mind of a mortal being. To live through the memories of others is a waste of the life I have been given, and I must believe that my birth as a Siyeen has significance of its own. But there are times when I need more knowledge that I possess, and it is to the island that I go.

Besides, even through the greatest efforts of my will, I cannot find the island. When my need is great, the island finds me.

I reach the island without remembering how, and immediately drop, exhausted, amongst the bones of my ancient forebear.

Huntara has the willowy form of a woodland deer and the expression on her face is the same expression I have seen on a deer who sees Uraun the moment before he looses the arrow.

What does she fear?

She slides through the shadows of the forest, her deep copper skin blending with the mottled browns and greens of the landscape, as though she is a woman molded from the brown clay of the riverbank and given the breath of life. She glances behind her once, twice, her breath snagging in her throat as her soundless steps advance deeper into the shadows of the wood. A still puddle has pooled where a tree's roots were torn from the ground many seasons ago, and as Huntara slips past the water, I glimpse her reflection.

My heart freezes.

The woman in the reflection is tearing into two. The one woman breathes darkness from her lips, her body wreathed in malice like smoke. The other woman shines with a radiance almost too powerful to behold and carries a strung bow with an arrow nocked, its head glittering like new-fallen snow.

I have never seen such intensity of conflict in the face of a human heart before. What has she come to do?

Huntara reaches the same place where she and I met first, and seats herself on the fallen log whose moss cushions her rest. She closes her eyes and waits, just as she had when I first saw her.

I realize, with a jolt, that she was not seeking solitude when I happened upon her. She was waiting for someone, and it was not for me.

She waits, her eyes closed, and the battle rages across her brow—the flicker of pain as she contemplates some deep trouble, the smoothness of resolve.

The forest crackles and Huntara summons her breath. Then she opens her eyes and remains still as three men enter her vision.

Her father. Her eldest brother. Her uncle.

"Huntara," the Sarudi chieftain speaks her name as one might speak to a favorite dog. Even in my dream, my blood prickles with indignation.

"Father," replies Huntara softly, with bowed head.

"You did well."

Huntara lifts her eyes to her father's for a moment, then drops them away.

"Did you do exactly as I told you, Huntara?"

"Yes."

"You did not accuse outright? This must not be traced back to you, or he will begin to suspect me."

"No. I only planted the suspicion but did not accuse directly."

"The Sarudi shall sing of you, Huntara, for generations to come."

"Shall they?" Huntara lifts her eyes, blooms of pink emerging in her pale cheeks. "People died."

"What did you think would happen? They were witnesses and could not be suffered to tell what they knew. And there were only three."

Huntara remains still and quiet.

"We are ready for the next stage," the Sarudi chieftain says quietly.

"What is that?"

"You will tell Uraun how the Siyeen chased you and you escaped with your life. Make it convincing. If necessary, burn yourself." When she did not respond, he growled, "I trust you will do what must be done for your people, Huntara."

Something rises in her eyes like a reflection, but it is a reflection from within, not from without. For a moment, I need no reflection to tell me which of the two beings inside her has won.

The skin of her face is shining as though lit from within.

"No," she whispers. Her body trembles like a leaf in wind, but her voice holds the immovable weight of a boulder.

"No," she says louder, as the men of her family gape at her. "If I cannot be loyal to the truth, to whom can I be loyal? There are some things I cannot do. Risha is a truth-wearer and Uraun is my husband."

"And I am your father," the chieftain snaps, spittle flying from his lips, his arms trembling. "You have put your hand to the bow. You cannot draw back now."

"I can," Huntara says, rising, her lips white but her posture resolute. "Find another deceiver. I will not meet you again."

The Sarudi chieftain springs upon his daughter with the snarl of a devouring beast, and his blows fall without care for her weaponlessness. "You cursed woman! You traitor! You are no daughter of mine! You destroy your people with your cowardice!"

Huntara screams, a sound the like of which I have never heard but which cleaves me down the spine like the stroke of a blade.

Huntara! You tried to tell me and I failed to see the truth you wore. Do not say I am too late.

FIFTEEN

THE FACE OF A BROTHER

My wings beat the air with strokes like claps of thunder and the sky-dark roils around me. The tips of the dead tree branches light in lavender as I pass, for my eyes burn with a fierce brilliance as heat pours from every scale on my body. Even my reflection explodes on the surface of the water with white fire.

Marsh, river, forest—I swallow all in the fury of my haste until I sense the nearness of my object and drop from the sky like a stone, wings folded against my blazing sides. As I drop, I scream, and the very air quakes like a solid thing at the sound of my war-cry.

The Sarudi chieftain's hand freezes in midstroke and I see that the fingernails are already black with the blood of his daughter. The other

127

two warriors scramble away from the fallen woman like creatures surprised in their den, hiding their treacherous hands and torn between instincts to fight or to flee.

It will make no difference to me. If they have killed Huntara, they are all dead men.

The trees explode with the violence of my wrath as I fall from the sky.

The three Sarudi warriors scatter with cries of terror.

Huntara deserves life more than her attackers deserve death. I overshadow her with my wings and scream the wrath of my protection to the backs of the retreating Sarudi. When I am certain they are gone, I turn to Huntara as a man, bleeding from the claws of the forest and the haste of my war.

My brother's wife lies crumpled upon the earth, her hair matted with her own blood and the tatters of moldering leaves, her body contracted against the murderous rage of her father.

I drop to my knees beside her, terrified to touch her, lest I should do more harm.

Where the shining woman stood in Huntara's eyes, there stands now only a pale being, like frost.

Death.

She was dead even before I could save her.

I should kill them—I should spill their blood as they spilled hers—but I can only sit and grieve as I have never grieved before.

I know now what I should have known. The Sarudi did not forget the Siyeen that put them to flight many years ago when they taunted two Karagi boys. They did not forget the Siyeen that wasted their warriors and stole their victory three times. They remembered and they sought its destruction.

The Siyeen cannot be taken by force, but it can be made vulnerable. So they sent the gentlest of their creatures—the daughter of their chieftain—to do what no warrior could do: to fill the mind of the Siyeen's brother with suspicions and lies. The Sarudi then ensured their case with subtlety. A few murdered Sarudi to establish Uraun's protection of the Sarudi, the mysterious burning of a village home: all become easily explained by the presence of an unpredictable creature. The Siyeen is dangerous, even to the Karagi who raised it.

The Sarudi are no longer the enemy.

The Siyeen is the enemy.

And Uraun listens and believes.

I wait by Huntara until the forest fills with the crackle of many footsteps. I am too weary with grief to move.

"There he is!"

That voice. My head snaps up and alarm slices through my veins.

"There he is," says the Sarudi chieftain again, and lifts his voice in a wail. "Aaaiiieee! Creature of death, what have you done to my daughter?"

But I hardly hear him as my eyes lock upon a face just behind him.

It is the first time I have seen my brother face-to-face since I left.

My brother's voice cracks on his words. "What have you done?"

He dashes forward and I withdraw as he drops next to his wife and reads in her expression all that I dare not tell him. For a moment, he can say and do nothing, only choke over his own breath, his fingers stiffening into claws as though to hold him to the earth.

"Take him!" shouts the Sarudi chieftain. "He is only a man now. Take the Siyeen before he can kill again."

I feel no fury, nor fear, nor desperation. I only feel the sudden weight of the inevitable. A stillness overtakes me and in that stillness, the memory of the wise woman speaks.

"I will tell you what must be—and also what *may* be."

The warriors dart forward, half-brave, half-ready to flee. I lift my hand and they skitter to a halt.

"Do not touch me," I say quietly. Then I turn and stride away and they do not pursue for the space of many breaths. Then, even with my back turned, I sense Uraun suddenly leap to his feet and take up his bow.

But his arrow never finds me.

I know how to evade hunters. I have spent the last seven years learning how to become invisible.

I know they are here when the shy fish near my rocky perch startle away. The marsh waters shudder with some disturbance, and I hear the distant sounds of footsteps. There is no pretense at quiet, and this concerns me. Cautiously, I creep closer and my heart leaps like the goatskin head of a struck war-drum. I see what I have long feared: a fully-armed hunting party of Karagi and Sarudi, some with spears, some with bows, and others with torches of burning pitch.

Uraun leads them, his eyes burning with grief and blood-lust.

"Is it not enough that I lose my father?" he rages to the murky waters. "Is it not enough that I lose my mother? But you will kill my wife also?"

How can I explain to my brother that the Sarudi are willing to carry their plan even this far, even to murder the woman who first set their deceptive design in motion, and to cast the blame upon the outcast Siyeen? They know my brother well. Blood begets blood in Uraun. But to convince Uraun of the depth of the Sarudi treachery? I would need greater power than that of the Siyeen.

They pursue me for three days, and everywhere I turn, I am harried and hemmed in. They know which ways I will try to escape, and they have laid traps in the waters. I am too sharp-eyed to miss them, but I am not small enough to avoid them. My shape will not conform to what I wish, but only to what I feel, and as much as I wish to be invisible, I feel only like a hunted monster, so that is the form I take, a slinking form with shifting eyes. If my pursuers see me in this form, they will feel justified in their purpose.

My enemies beat the waters, and pour out some deadly concoction that burns like oil upon the surface of the waters. There is no refuge for me and my strength wanes. My time runs like shadows chased across the grass by the sun, and I taste death in the back of my raw throat. I know that Uraun will not relent this time.

It is at evening that he finds me, and I plead for my life.

"Uraun! Please."

"A child?" one man asks. Yes, a child. Uraun would know its face: the child who waited for a father who never returned, so many years ago.

"It is an illusion," Urawn says, and draws back his bowstring.

I glance toward the waters, but there are no wings now. The Siyeen—Nayu, perhaps?—has already given me my second chance to live, and that second life has only deepened my sorrow. I have found no answers. I have not undone my mistakes, for I did not know how without making other mistakes.

It has all been for nothing.

Then I notice the reflections and see what I had not seen before.

Uraun's reflection weeps and blood pours from a wound at his heart. He weeps for his wife, but I know he weeps also for me, for our mother, our father, our people, our separation.

Behind him, all the Karagi aim their weapons at my heart and their reflections show warriors— some bolder, some more fearful, but all true. They have always been true.

And the Sarudi? In life, their arrows and spears aim also at me, but in the reflections, their prey is Uraun.

I am not their object. This hunt was never meant for me. The Sarudi will use the confusion of the hunt and of my last struggle for life as an occasion to strike down the Karagi chieftain. Thus they will be rid of me and rid of Uraun in one day.

The Sarudi hunt Uraun.

And I know now what I may do, with this second life given to me. Many years ago, the wise woman spoke the truth of what may happen to me, and somehow, I am no longer afraid of it.

I know which way the arrow will fly. I am ready for it.

When I hear its whisper, I step firmly into its path.

The pain does not follow as quickly as I expect. For a moment, I stare blankly at the shaft that emerges from my chest, and at the blood pooling around the puncture, blossoming like a scarlet flower from my rawhide tunic. If it were not for the evidence of sight and the impact I felt, I would hardly believe I am hit.

Then I choke on blood, my heart lurches sideways, and panic drowns every other consideration.

I do not want to die.

I do not want to die.

I do not want to die.

Then follows the unbearable heartbreak: my brother has killed me.

But I have a task yet to perform, and all will be in vain if I fail. I can feel the inevitable transformation. I have been many forms, especially the land-Siyeen by which I am known, but I have never yet become the water-Siyeen, the opalescent white eel with fins like wings.

I sense the tingle in my hands as webs grow between my fingers, the slipperiness of my skin as it changes to glittering opalescent white, the twisting and melting together of my legs, the explosion from my shoulders and back as wing-like fins unfold toward the sky. I am becoming what I am at heart: the Siyeen, bearer of truth.

I have none of the hard scales of the land-Siyeen, for the true Siyeen is vulnerable. Many arrows pierce me, but I hardly feel them now. I have only one object.

Uraun's bow releases again and again, each arrow wounding me anew, but I will not be shaken from my purpose. With a flicker of movement as quick as thought, I wrap the coils of my bleeding body around him, turn, and plunge into the waters.

The blood pours from me now, and fear would make me lose my senses, were it not for the wise woman's words from long ago, speaking softly to me in my mind.

"You have seen from the legend of Nayu that the Siyeen has one gift that is greater than all other gifts. In life, the Siyeen cannot show others what it sees in them. It can only show its own self truly. But in death, the Siyeen can show another what it sees, and make another to see truly. When the last of its life-blood covers the one it loves, that person will become like the Siyeen, knowing the truth."

Uraun, Uraun, in my death I am saving you. You have listened to a lie, and chosen it above the truth you saw in me, but I will not leave you to be slain by it. I will die to set you free. I will die to make you my brother once more.

SIXTEEN

A SECOND LIFE

Something has happened to me. I stroke toward the glitter of light at the surface, and purple infuses the waters around me. My lungs burst for air and heat pounds in my head.

I explode from the surface and fling back my long black hair, choking for breath.

The Karagi and Sarudi wait at the edge of the depths, shaken.

"Uraun, you're alive!" my cousin gasps. "When the Siyeen took you, I feared you were gone forever."

"How did you manage to escape?" my brother-in-law asks, and his question seems sharper than I would expect.

"I did not escape," I reply, swimming toward them with ragged, exhausted strokes. "The Siyeen freed me."

My brethren reach to pull me onto the higher ground, a strange sight freezes me.

What is this? Have I gone mad?

My cousin's reflection ripples with the face and body of a bear, brutish but with a solidity of purpose and will that can be trusted. Another Karagi warrior is accompanied by a thin reflection, and I know that he is bendable to another's will, desperate to please me, to be accepted. A third Karagi warrior has a form like stone, inflexible, but his heart pulses with a slow, steady light, and remains moldable.

I have never seen my men in this way. They are flawed and crude, but they are true.

But the reflections of the Sarudi show the faces of serpents ready to strike, and though in life they make a show of solidarity with the Karagi and of deference toward me, in the reflections, their arrows are trained upon me and upon every one of my faithful Karagi.

When my cousin bends to pull me up, I whisper a command to him. He blinks, but my gaze holds his, unshakable. Then his eyes widen and his whisper is hoarse with fear.

"Uraun, your eyes!"

But I have already seen it. In the reflection of my cousin's eyes, I recognize my own face: the crooked nose from many mishaps, the scar along one cheek, the high cheekbones. It must be a trick of the light, but it seems as though my eyes are no longer black, but a shining purple.

I gain my footing and my cousin slips back amongst the hunters and quietly relays my command.

"Is it truly dead?" My Sarudi brother-in-law probes the depths of the dark waters with the tip of his spear. "Perhaps it is simply a trick, to put us off our guard."

"The Siyeen is not a treacherous creature," I say behind him. "Not like you."

The man whirls but my arrow finds its mark before he can so much as lift his spear-tip. Behind me, the marshes explode with frenzied footsteps, the hiss of arrows, and the grunts of men embattled for their lives. Seven Sarudi fall to the Karagi before they realize that the hunt has turned against them.

My warriors cluster round me and two fall to the ferocity of the Sarudi before we tighten our defense and begin to strike back.

The Sarudi outnumber us two to one. How could I have been so blind as to let such a force mingle with my own warriors? Ah, but deception deceives itself. If I had desired the truth, I would have gained wisdom as well. Despite our disadvantage, my faithful Karagi do not hesitate and neither do I. I am their chieftain, and I lead with the ferocity of a Siyeen.

The struggle is fierce, and in the end, many of my men lie, sightless and drifting amongst the marsh weeds, but not one of the Sarudi has escaped with his life.

"I cannot believe it." My cousin drops to the ground and covers his head with his hands. "We won. We won. I still do not know how." He raises his eyes to me, a question heavy in his gaze. "How did you know, Uraun?"

Now I know why Risha hardly knew how to tell me what he saw. The truth is simple and clear, but it is so difficult to show to those who do not seek for it with their whole hearts.

I trace the scar upon my cheek and reply quietly, "It is enough that I knew. I will have dealings with liars no longer, for I will be a chieftain of nobility and truth."

As we leave the Sarudi dead to the scavengers of the marshes, and bear our own dead and wounded back to the boats we have tied some distance away, I turn, heart-weary, to catch a last glimpse of the waters where my brother never rose. I know now the truth in him, and my heart smites me at what I have done.

Risha, you were not worthy of death.

As if in answer, I catch a momentary glimpse of something white just under the surface. It is so strange, I hardly know what to think, but I could swear I see an uplifted wing, as though raised in blessing or in a final farewell.

They say if you see wings beneath the water, you get a second chance to live. If that is true, I will use my second life well.

Other science fiction and fantasy titles
by Yaasha Moriah:

IMMERSION
PROJECT MINERVA
PROMETHEUS
REFLECTIONS

Find out more about the author and upcoming books
online at www.YaashaMoriah.com.

Facebook: Yaasha Moriah
Twitter: @YaashaMoriah